SALVAGED

SHANNA M. HEATH

To my beautiful family,
Jeff, Abigail, Miriam, and Owen.

Contents

CHAPTER 1

The Only Constant Is Change

»» ———————— ««

"Metastasized" is now my least favorite word. It's not even an ACT Word of the Day study term. I should have known something was wrong the minute I got Nonny's text:

Hadley, we need to talk about something important at dinner.

Then her second one an hour later.

I'd been enjoying a giant bacon cheeseburger at Puckett's on the Chesapeake Bay with Taylor, my best friend, when my phone chimed. That was hours ago, when my biggest concerns were avoiding the double dates Taylor keeps insisting on and obsessing over an internship at the Naval Research Lab I want next summer. At least that low-level anxiety came with a side of chili-cheese fries.

It was Nonny's third text that sent me hurrying home through Annapolis' historic district, past brick colonial buildings and cobbled streets. Now, I take the steps two at a time up to the Tudor-style home we live in. I enter the arched doorway to the rhythmic thump, thump, thump of Nonny at her sewing machine. Nothing can be all that bad if she's working on a project, right? After dropping my shoulder bag on the front bench, I take a steadying breath to calm myself, then saunter across the hardwood floor to a table where she pieces together a quilt.

"Hey, Nonny." I wipe my palms on my shorts in a feeble attempt to quiet my nerves.

She puffs a strand of errant salt-n-pepper gray from her face and offers a quick smile. "Hey sweetheart. Let me finish this up and we'll talk while we prep for dinner." Why is she avoiding eye contact?

"Any mail for me today?" I'm so hopeful for any information about the internship that I have a hard time waiting for her response. The program is important to me—I really want to honor my grandfather's legacy. My grandpa, the Captain, was a well-loved math professor at the Naval Academy. I pick at my pinky nail while I wait out the hour-long second she takes to answer.

"No ma'am." She smiles at me. "You keep waiting on the good Lord's timing. All things work together for our good and His Glory."

I offer a half-hearted attempt at a smile to let Nonny know I appreciate her positive perspective, hiding my disappointment at the lack of news. Nonny gestures upstairs. "You go get cleaned up, then set the table while I straighten up my mess."

Nothing could be that bad if she didn't tell me as soon as I came in, I remind myself. Might be time to suggest Nonny start future texts with, "Not an emergency, but…"

I reclaim my bag, climb the stairs, and head to my bedroom. I toss my bag on my twin size, quilt-covered bed and plop down at my desk. Scattered around my corkboard are pictures of my life, laid out like an exhibit at a museum. Images of me with my birth mom, who I haven't seen since she left us when I was three years old. Pictures of me smiling with the Captain at a Navy Day celebration when I was seven, our last together. There's one of me standing next to Taylor from the first day of cross-country try-outs in sixth grade. We'd just met, and we were all elbows and metal grins back then. Dozens more show me and Taylor at various cross-country meets, school dances, and church events from Vacation Bible School to youth group overnights and everything in between. I ache for the day I can pin an acceptance letter next to them.

After kicking off my sandals, I head to the bathroom to wash up, throw my shoulder-length, dirty-blonde ponytail into a messy bun, and splash some cold water on my face. Supposedly, my resemblance to my mom is uncanny. Same color hair, same almond-shaped eyes, and the same sprinkle of freckles across the bridge of my nose. I'll take Nonny's word for it. My mom was only sixteen when she had me. It's hard to remember what she looked like, so that old polaroid is as close as I'll get.

The sound of Nonny digging through the pots and pans pulls me from my reverie and I'm lured downstairs by the promise of her famous chicken and dumplings. I finish setting the placemats and silverware on our small kitchen table, then help her roll out the dumplings and shred the chicken.

As the dish simmers, I squish a frozen can of concentrated lemonade slush into a glass pitcher, where it thunks unceremoniously on the bottom. I mix it with water, pour two glasses, and settle into my seat. Once our plates are ready, I admire the spread in front of us. The creamy entree, the yeast rolls with cinnamon butter. There's even a chocolate cream pie. It smells heavenly. We fill our plates and bow our heads as Nonny prays.

I lift my head as she finishes the blessing. "Dawna Edwards, you have outdone yourself." I rub my hands together, eager to dig in.

She purses her lips, annoyed that I've used her proper name. But Nonny takes the compliment—she knows this meal is my favorite. It's comfort food, my self-proclaimed love language, and Nonny is fluent.

Three bites into dinner, I open my mouth to broach the text subject, deciding I might as well get it over with. She clears her throat and beats me to it. "Hadley, I had a check-up at the doctor's office today."

I nod. This isn't new. Nonny's had breast cancer for years, but it has always been stable. And she has check-ups all the time. Definitely not something to garner three texts and leave me on edge all afternoon.

"Everything okay? You're alright, right?" She doesn't answer and averts her gaze. I squirm in my seat as I wait, but still nothing. I set my fork down and sit up a little straighter. "Nonny. What is it?"

She sips a bit of her lemonade and then looks me straight in the eyes. "I got unsettling news from some recent pathology reports."

The food I swallow struggles to get past the lump in my throat. This doesn't sound great and I'm certain this can't be right. Nonny's fought this cancer like a boss, in my humble opinion, and maintained good health despite her diagnosis.

"Bloodwork from a recent visit showed abnormal blood cell counts. Dr. Stein ran a few tests, and they determined the cancer has metastasized to my bones."

"Meta-whata?" Maybe I have heard this word before but wasn't willing to accept it could even happen to her. Not to my Nonny. My lungs tighten and there isn't enough air in the room.

"The cancer has spread and I've stopped responding to treatments, Hadley. I have to consider my other options. *Your* other options."

"W-what? What does that mean?" My voice sounds foreign to my own ears.

Nonny sighs. "It means I'll need more care, and it isn't fair for me to expect a sixteen-year-old to offer it. Treatments aren't working, and even medicine that might work will likely be harder on my body than the cancer. When the time comes, I'll take enough medicine to manage any pain and keep me comfortable. I won't be able to stay home, Hadley. It won't be an option."

"No, Nonny, no." I shake my head. "You're the strongest person I know. What if the reports are wrong?" My voice rises, but I can't seem to help myself. "Why can't you stay home? I'm here. Sometimes Aunt Rose comes to stay. Could she help?"

"Hadley, Aunt Rose hasn't been here since the Captain passed away. I need you to understand what I'm telling you. I know this is hard to hear." She reaches across the table and squeezes my hand. "We can't always control everything. We need to move closer to your family in Kentucky, sweetheart."

It takes me a few beats to process her words and I pull my hand back.

"What family in Kentucky?" I can't think of a single person I know in Kentucky. I wonder if this is how it feels to be thrown in the middle of a twisted episode of *Pranked* or *Twilight Zone.*

"Your father and his family live in Kentucky." Her words come out gentle, cautious, as if I might not hear her. I blink. My father? She's throwing information at me faster than I can handle. My chest tightens. My grandmother is sick with so little time left. This must be bad if she's finally telling me about my dad.

I'm also beyond disgusted with myself because for a half-second I actually thought about losing any possible shot at the internship. How could I be so selfish?

"How long have you known? About the cancer? And my dad? You know my father?" We never talk about this taboo subject.

"Of course, dear. Of course." She takes a deep breath and I see a flash of pain cross her face. "When we found out your mother was pregnant, the Captain put in for a transfer. He had such fond memories of his time in the Navy, and when the professorship at the Academy opened, it came at a very opportune time. Your father didn't know about your mother's pregnancy when we left, and we thought it best to keep it that way. He's only known about you for a few months. He is eager to meet you. He and his family have prepared a space for you."

I scoff. "Oh, that's nice. What if he doesn't want me living with him, Nonny? Have you thought about that?" I hate the way I sound, so desperate and snarky. But he has a *family*.

"Your father is a very kind man. He was a bit taken aback when I called, but we've spoken at length several times."

"How is it you've spoken to him 'at length?' You told me you just found this out."

"I'm sorry Hadley. I've known longer than I let on. I didn't know how or when to tell you. With the realtor coming tomorrow I couldn't put it off any longer."

That leaves my mouth hanging open. "When?" I demand. "When are we supposed to move?"

"Two weeks from yesterday. The house is going up for sale tomorrow."

I drop my fork. How could she? My world turns upside down and the only thing I think to do is flee upstairs, my appetite for Nonny's famous chicken and dumplings lost.

CHAPTER 2

Postponing the Inevitable

»» ———————————— «««

A lone ray of sunshine peeks through the blinds and wakes me the next morning. The soft sheets tempt me to roll over and relish the relaxing comfort, until the sorrowful conversation from the night before overwhelms me. I reach for my phone to check the time, but the movement causes my head to ache in that tragic I-cried-myself-to-sleep kind of way. Taylor always says I must be thinking of rainbows and unicorns half the time, so this whole dark sadness stuff makes my stomach roll.

I'm supposed to meet Taylor in half an hour for a run. She'll know something's up as soon as she sees my puffy eyes and I can't force myself to share this news with her yet. I'm not a superstitious person but saying certain things out loud makes them too real, gives them power. And I'm too numb for anything to feel more real right now. This pain is fresh. So, I shoot her a text:

So sorry, can't make our run. Killer cramps this a.m.

I don't wait to see how she responds. Her persuasive powers can't change my mind if I don't see her return message. Instead, it's up and at 'em while I pretend I didn't just blow off my best-friend. I throw on some workout shorts and a tank top to make friends with the treadmill in our basement. I might not be ready to hit the pavement with Taylor, but I can at least run off some anxiety before breakfast. Dreadmill it is. Bring on some endorphins cause heaven knows I could use them.

After conquering a half hour of running in place, I spend an embarrassing amount of time contemplating life under the showerhead, as if it might rain down solutions to my problems while rinsing the shampoo from my scalp. I drag myself out, dry off, and comb my damp hair. Then I twist it into a claw and slip on a faded Washington Wizards tee and some cut-offs. I check my reflection in the mirror then decide I don't care what I look like. Barefoot, I tread to the kitchen to pour myself a bowl of cereal. I pick at my Cinnamon Toast Crunch with a spoon until it becomes a soggy mush, then feel bad because what kind of monster wastes awesome cereal?

The rest of the morning is a real chore. As I clean up after breakfast, I hear Nonny clear her throat behind me only to turn and see her push a copy of the book *When Your Parent Has Cancer* across the island. That better not be required reading. Why can't Nonny let me enjoy my denial? I'll be hiding that in the bottom of my desk drawer as soon as possible. Or burning it.

"Hadley, grab some shoes. The realtor should be here any minute." Oh gosh. *Not* my idea of fun.

To be honest, the realtor is pretty nice. Mrs. Willow helps Nonny assess the value of the home to determine a selling price, and decide what necessary repairs and upgrades we need, all that kind of stuff. Nonny gives her best passive-aggressive stink eye when we check out my room and she sees my unmade bed.

Sorry Nonny, but apathy wouldn't allow me to turn down my sheets this morning. In our living room, we each claim a seat around the coffee table, and when they start with the boring old people talk, I zone out because my brain is elsewhere. I sense the beginnings of an upset stomach when the realtor asks where we're planning to move.

Unphased, Nonny gives this woman the whole run-down in her typical matter-of-fact manner, and based on her look of concern sent in my direction, I get the feeling she's spelling it all out for my ears, not Mrs. Willow's. Forcing me to accept it, I guess. To this woman's credit, she doesn't bat an eye, just nods in sympathy during the whole sad tale. We walk her out to her SUV where she takes a giant "For Sale" sign out of the back, then stakes it into the beautiful flower lot my Nonny works so hard on. Sounds a whole lot like the stake driving right through my broken heart.

"I suspect your beautiful home will sell quickly, what with the seller's market and all. And in the historic district, too."

Ok, maybe I don't like her as much as I did at first. I don't want our house to sell fast. I want to stay here. This is my home. The only home I've ever known. Mrs. Willow packs her tablet away in her oversized, designer purse. "Ladies, I've got a date with a duplex on the other side of town. It's been a pleasure."

Oh no, the date. I promised Taylor I'd go out with her, her boyfriend, and some random guy she's so bent on setting me up with. Here comes another copout text to Taylor:

Stomach bug hit the Naval lab. Picking up an extra shift tonight to help out. So sorry to miss the date!

I'm not sorry to miss the date, but ugh, I'm gonna burn for all these lies.

"Well, that wasn't so bad, was it?" Nonny looks at me with hopeful, probing eyes. I want to love all the cancer cells right out of her, so I nod my head in agreement to make her happy.

"I suppose there's no time like the present to get started on our to-do list. Would you please head to the hardware store to pick up packing boxes and some tape?" She hands me a list of items to purchase and some money. I stare at her handwriting on the crinkled list–strong and with a feminine flare, just like her. This doesn't look like the penmanship of someone slowly fading away.

No, I do not want to go to the hardware store. I want to go back to the doctor and force him to comb through Nonny's charts to figure out what mistake he's made. Nonny *can't* be this sick. None of this packing/moving/changing every single part of my entire life business needs to happen.

But I love my Nonny and my self-diagnosed allergy to confrontation prevents me from arguing, so it's off to the hardware store for me. Begrudgingly, I kick on my sandals, grab my bag, and slump out the door.

###

Sunday after church, I meet Taylor at Puckett's for lunch. To say I've been avoiding her is an understatement. Confession: I even called to take an extra shift at the lab to turn at least one lie into a truth. Those lies piled on to my sensitive guilt—guilt that pricks at my heart and have some serious emotional consequences. Like I need more emotions to process.

Puckett's Grille has an eclectic variety of cool, nostalgic signs all over the brick walls of their restaurant. The one next to my seat seems pretty deep for a casual dining place and reads *"The Only Constant is Change."* Psh. Before yesterday, my life was nothing but constant. Wake up, run, volunteer at the Navy Pier, work, shower, sleep, repeat. Some steady combination of these, even now, during summer when I don't have school, yet another constant.

"Did you know you get this deep line in the middle of your brows when you concentrate? A scowl like that might scare a girl off if she didn't know you well." Taylor doesn't mince words.

"Great, now I can add premature wrinkles to my list of worries." I stop my contemplation long enough to drag a hot, salty fry through ketchup.

"You know what? When you get that internship at the Office of Naval Research, we can meet for impromptu afternoon snacks here all the time." She clears her throat when I don't respond. I nod to encourage her to continue. "You're too serious this afternoon. And you're a total shoo-in for that internship. Are you doubling with me and Josh Friday?" That look in her eyes is entirely too hopeful and does nothing to ease the nagging panic in the back of my mind.

"What does Nonny think about your chances? And don't assume I'm letting you avoid the date conversation again. I know you're stalling." She has no idea. "Don't get mad at me for asking, but have you thought of a Plan B if the Naval internship doesn't work out?"

Yep, time to come clean. This is too hard.

"Hadley? It's not like you'll have to apply to Monsters University if you don't get the internship. And you can

14

borrow my amber tear-drop earrings for the date. They would totally make your hazel eyes pop. Oh! Or the sapphire studs would look amazing with your blonde hair. Hadley, are you ignoring me?"

That snaps me out of my trance, but Taylor's expression is hard to read.

"No. No, I'm sorry. I'm not ignoring you." She snorts and raises an eyebrow. I can't help the way my eyes get misty when I start to speak, and my voice cracks.

"Nonny is sick, Taylor."

Taylor's eyebrows furrow. She sits up straighter, her concern evident. "What do you mean? Did she start a new cancer medication that's making her sick? Or did she catch that stomach bug or something?"

I shake my head and choke out a whisper. "It's her cancer. It's bad, Taylor. We have to move."

"Oh, Hadley, I am so sorry." Her eyes pool with tears that threaten to spill over as she reaches for my hand. I've never been the touchy-feely type, and often scoff at physical contact, especially if I'm upset, but I don't jerk my hand away this time. I fill Taylor in on Nonny's prognosis, even using the dreaded T-word, "*terminal*," that I couldn't bring myself to think about just yesterday.

"That's not all." Oh boy, deep breath. "I'mmovingtoKentuckytolivewithmydad." I rip off the metaphorical Band-Aid to get that out before I can't. Taylor's jaw goes slack when I continue to tell her about my father and his family.

"Nonny is moving to an assisted living facility in Broadwater, Kentucky. I will stay with Greg–my dad. He has two kids and a wife." My shoulders sag in agonizing defeat.

Taylor says little, only offering an occasional "uh-huh" or head nod to encourage me to continue, but I know she needs time to process all that I've told her. Heck, *I* need more time to process all that I've told her. Both of us seem to have lost our appetite and our food remains untouched. If disregarded food isn't a red flag, what is?

After a silence that stretches forever, Taylor switches to a more upbeat tone. "I am so going to visit you."

I snort. "Broadwater is over 600 miles from Annapolis."

She mock snorts in return. "Airplanes, friend. Airplanes."

I'm happy to pretend, at least for the moment, that her paychecks from her part time job at Chesapeake Charms are enough for airfare.

###

Maybe I was wrong when I said speaking about something out loud gave it more power. It was a massive relief to talk to Taylor and it's nice to have a friend to confide in. On Monday, she comes over to help me pack non-essentials like off-season clothes and whatnot. Nonny hired an auction house to sell most of our furniture and movers for the rest of our things. Rolls of packing tape and bubble wrap are everywhere, and cardboard boxes lie scattered over the hardwood floor in my bedroom.

Taylor steps over a box and reaches for the bookshelf. "I guess you should pack everything you won't immediately need?"

"Then why are you about to pack my books?" I mean, surely Taylor knows me better.

"Good point." She sets my copy of Jenny B. Jones' *There You'll Find Me* back on the

shelf and moves to my closet. "Maybe we could start with your picture frames or winter clothes? Hadley?"

I sigh, frustrated that I have to do any of this at all. I don't want to move and I sure as heck don't want to think of life without Nonny. Too many big changes all at once. New state, new school, new family. I need a t-shirt that says "overwhelmed." Talk about sipping from the firehose. I sit on the edge of my bed and, heaven help me, tear up.

"Whoa, whoa, whoa. Lemme just stop you right there." Taylor plops down next to me and starts to say something, but reconsiders. "You know what, on second thought, let it out." Bless her heart, she tears up too.

We're both a blubbery mess when Nonny comes in. She takes one look at us and shakes her head.

"Girls! What in the world?" She tsks us (actually *tsks us!*), "Now, now, none of that." But her voice betrays her sympathy. She wiggles her hips right down between us and wraps an arm around each of our shoulders. She reaches around to grabs a box of tissues from the nightstand and Taylor and I obediently take one.

"The mood seems too heavy in here. We need chili fries at Puckett's, my treat." Did my ears break right along with my heart? I heard what she said but Nonny has never ordered chili fries in her life. I see the sacrifice she's making, and I approve.

"You talked me into it." Taylor hops up, wipes her eyes on her sleeves, and tosses me my bag. We go to Puckett's and attack those chili fries like we've got a personal vendetta against awesome food. We are not to be judged. Everyone is allowed to eat their feelings when cancer is involved.

###

It's two days before D-day (read: moving day). Taylor, several of my closest friends from youth group, and even a few colleagues from the Naval Research Center gather at Puckett's for a going-away party. A huge spread of appetizers and desserts lay before us: potato skins, quesadilla triangles, brownie bites, and cheesecake bars.

My friends know how to send someone away in style. My naval friends brought table decorations, like tablecloths that read "Bon Voyage," and little battleship centerpieces. I can't help but smile at the cheesiness of the theme.

I gorge myself on all things fried or chocolate, then gifts are pushed my way. I unwrap a photo book, a keychain shaped like Kentucky (which would be cooler if it had keys to a car attached, but whatevs), a journal, and a bunch of gift cards to Kentucky Fried Chicken. My friends must think I need to naturalize myself to my new home. By the time I've opened all their cards, I have nine $10 gift certificates. Maybe I can win the insta-fam over with Colonel Sanders' secret recipe. Worth a shot.

I open Taylor's gift last. I shuffle through a mass of tissue paper to find a box of twelve dated letters and a Chesapeake Charms necklace I'm sure she made. Our eyes meet and she's a bigger mess than I am. Heartbreaking tears stream down her face, but she smiles. I'll cherish these gifts forever.

She gestures to the envelopes. "So, these should last you a year. I tried to write down happy memories and a few special things we'll miss now that we won't be as close, in proximity at least. Every time you open a letter it will be like getting a warm hug straight from me. I mean, I know you hate hugs, but whatever. I'm rambling."

I smile and take a closer look at the necklace. How in the world?

"I cut a circle of the Puckett's logo from one of their coasters and used epoxy resin to make a pendant. Stuck that bad boy on a cross chain and 'viola.' Do you like it?" She looks almost bashful as she waits for my approval.

"No, I don't like it. I love it." It's quirky and artsy and 100 percent authentic, just like her. I suck it up and hug her. Worth it.

Now I just need a gift that will help me pack the rest of my boxes. And a cure for breast cancer.

CHAPTER 3

Leavin' on a Jet Plane

»» ———————————— ««

I've flown plenty of times before—to Hawaii on vacation, to Whiting Field in Florida, to a distant cousin's wedding up North—but those flights were different than this one. For one thing, those flights had a temporary destination, and they were round-trip.

This is final. Permanent.

There's more turbulence in my stomach than on the plane as I battle anxiety about all that awaits me in Kentucky. I read the same magazines several times over and regret not digging a book out of a packed box before the moving company drove off. Nonny is asleep and I can't bring myself to wake her. I put in my earbuds and listen to *Pi Takes the Cake* my favorite podcast for teens like me who enjoy the science of numbers. Two young hosts discuss how math is relevant to all things pop-culture, from math trending in television and print—think Numb3rs, Big Bang Theory, and the entire Avengers/Marvel series— to sports, music, and celebrity geeks. Did you know Michael Jordan is a huge fan of math? There's an entire episode about him.

I attempt to distract myself until the flight attendant brings my complimentary snack and beverage (and by complimentary, the mathematician in me would like to point out that the cost of said beverage is built into my ticket…). If I don't find something to divert my attention from my current situation, I will go insane with worry over things I can't control. I do allow myself a few moments to consider what my father's reaction to me might be. Nonny explained that he's married and he and his wife have two young children, an eight-year-old little girl and a boy who just turned four. Am I about to crash their idyllic family? What if his wife hates me? If I throw a metaphorical wrench in the works, that would suck. Or what if she's a total momster? I shudder.

An unmistakable '*ding*' sounds overhead and the flight attendant instructs us to remain seated with our chairs in an upright position as we begin our descent. I pack the magazines away and tidy up my belongings, shoving my Airpods into my messenger bag and scramble to throw away snack wrappers. The kid in the seat behind me continues to kick the back of my chair and I offer up a silent prayer that my half-siblings aren't as annoying as he is. What if they're worse? Once we land, I give Nonny a gentle shake to wake her and stand to help her with the overhead luggage. My feet seem as if they're stuck in cement. I can't do this.

"You can do this, Hadley." Can Nonny read my mind? "One foot in front of the other."

"Right, of course." I toss my bag over my shoulder and walk off the plane, attempting my new telepathic abilities to communicate with the stewardess *"There has been a mistake. Take me back to Annapolis."* It seems I am not, in fact, telepathic. She smiles and welcomes me to Kentucky, home of horses, bourbon, and bluegrass. She's too chipper for my circumstances and I'm getting more apprehensive. I pinch the skin between my thumb and forefinger. Everything is out of place.

I don't realize I'm holding my breath until I step off the plane, but my neck is stiff and I'm not sure if it's because the seats were uncomfortable or if it's stress. I help Nonny with our carry-ons and trudge toward baggage claim. Maybe if I drag my feet slower, they'll think I decided not to come and drive away. I could be Nonny's roommate at assisted living.

And then it happens.

I spot a family of four with a dad who has my almond-shaped, hazel eyes. I turn slowly, unwilling to take another step, but Nonny won't allow it. In the center of the group stands a little girl with a stolen dimple holding a poster with glue and glitter that says, "WELCOME HADLEY!" A tiny little boy who must be my half-brother wipes snot with his hand. Nice. If I thought I felt uncomfortable, the guy who must be my father looks like he's about to get his teeth drilled. Sweat on his brow, ash-stricken face, stiff posture. I'm a Zen-master compared to him and somehow, this thought calms me. As odd as it is, my stepmom looks pretty chill. She has her auburn hair in a relaxed ponytail and wears a soft, friendly expression. All this despite a fidgeting, hangry preschooler at the first meeting with her husbands' illegitimate lovechild. So, there's that.

"Dawna, nice to see you." My father takes Nonny's bag with a look of concern on his face. I'm sure seeing his high school sweetheart's mother in declining health is hard. She's always been spunky and healthy, now she's terminal. I hate that word.

"Thank you, Greg. And you as well." Nonny's eyes grow misty, and when I look over at Greg, his have as well. He clears his throat but doesn't say much else to Nonny. To be fair, she did hide his daughter for over sixteen years.

Then his eyes find me and the color drains from his face.

"You are the spitting image of Jenny," he says in barely a whisper. Awkward. I'm sure his wife will delight in living with the clone of his ex. He shakes his head. "I'm sorry, Hadley, I wasn't quite prepared for such a striking resemblance. It's nice to meet you. And please, call me Greg." This moment is so surreal, I'm suddenly lightheaded. He extends a hand to shake and afterward, an uncomfortable silence rests between us. No one seems to know what to say.

Greg's wife clears her throat. "Hi, I'm Karie, and this is Libby, who is eight."

"Hi!" Libby squeaks, then her cheeks grow pink. I try to offer a reassuring smile, reminding myself this day isn't easy for her either.

"And this is our Patrick. He just turned four." Karie ruffles his soft brown curls, and the little boy attaches himself to his mom's leg, bashful.

"How was the flight? Can we help you with your things?" She reaches for Nonny's remaining baggage, and I can tell Nonny already likes Karie simply by the way she relaxes her posture. Nonny smiles at me, and my fake-telepathy decides she's giving me a pep-talk that conveys, "See, they're nice."

The jury is still out, Nonny.

They assist us as we unload our bags from the conveyor belt and help us to a black minivan, or "Swagger Wagon," as Karie informs me.

"Buckle up, buttercup!" Libby climbs in right beside me and grins. Okay, this kid has spunk. "I lost a tooth yesterday and I got two dollars this morning when I woke up." With obvious pride, she points to a gaping hole where an incisor used to be. Two dollars? They should make a new podcast about tooth fairy inflation on Pi Takes the Cake. Maybe Libby takes better care of her teeth than I do. I offer her my best smile and turn my attention to the glitter stuck to the skin of my thigh. It seems the poster shed some devil dust and it bred in the car during our airport meet and greet.

As we leave the Bluegrass Airport, I get my first taste of the bluegrass. Lexington seems pleasant enough. I mean, there are no chalk-outlined bodies, multiple burned down buildings, or shot-out streetlights. I'm being dramatic. I lean forward in my seat to take in a beautiful, sprawling horse park. In the forty-five minutes it takes to reach Broadwater, Nonny makes fast friends with Patrick in a riveting game of Go Fish. Libby informs me that we're in for a treat. Lunch will be at Chick-fil-A, land of the Lord's chicken, sweet iced tea, and a fun game called "*how-many-times-can-we-make-the-employees-say* '*my pleasure?*'"

According to Libby, I must order sweet tea. I take a sip of my new drink and, oh my, sweet tea is liquid diabetes. I love it the moment the sweet goodness passes my lips. I take another sip, then another. Where has this been all my life and how dare Nonny hide this from me? I shoot her a look.

"I let you try it when you were a toddler and you hated it. Never bothered to suggest it again." I've never felt so deprived. She raises a brow at my second refill and I already know we're going to have to stop before we make it to their home. My new home. And for the record, we tallied up eight "My pleasure's." Decent, on the authority of Libby.

###

The small town oozes with charm. Main Street seems to have personality. I make a mental note of a coffee shop, a bookstore, and several cute boutiques. But it isn't Annapolis. We pull into a quaint neighborhood and park in the drive of a Victorian style home with character, much different from the historic brownstone I shared with Nonny. There's a gated backyard with a swing-set and toys are strewn across the well-maintained front yard. A basketball rests by the steps, and a bubble mower chills on its side.

We park the swagger wagon in the driveway and enter through the backdoor. Backdoors are saved for close friends and family. And I'm family, it seems. Greg and Karie give me the grand tour of the place.

"We vacuumed for you!" Libby exclaims, and I can't help but smile at her faux pas. The living room is cozy, with its giant sectional couch. House plants and framed pictures with absolutely no one I recognize are scattered about. Their kitchen is awesome. Helllllllooo fancy Kitchen aid mixer. And their fridge is ginormous. I hope they don't mind that I enjoy cooking. Baking is cathartic.

When we get to the room they've prepared for me, I find that the walls have a fresh coat of white paint and are bare. I'm careful to hide my expression, but Karie must sense my apprehension.

"We weren't sure about your personal preferences or tastes, so we thought we'd let you get acquainted with your new space, and then you can pick out paint and pictures." Fair enough. I am digging the full-size bed with a pillowtop mattress, however. I've always had a twin bed at home, so that's kind of awesome. Karie inspects for invisible dust on the small but plain desk. "Your personal things should arrive from the moving company in a day or so. Then you can really make this space yours."

"My room is right across the hall!" Libby again. I like this insta-sis. I'm not all that picky about my walls, but NO GLITTER. Libby and Patrick are so excited to show me their rooms I'm downright honored. I enter a land of Legos, puzzles, and coloring books. A stack of board games two feet high fills one shelf in their playroom. I will destroy them in Exploding Kittens. Maybe I should wait until after my eighteenth birthday so they don't disown me too soon?

Greg clears his throat. "We should probably get Dawna moved into her apartment. I assume you'd like to go as well?"

My expression falls. I want to help Nonny move into her new place, but I wish I didn't have to. We sold our house, flew all the way to Kentucky, met my dad, and *this* is what makes it too real for me. I try to hide my misty eyes, but Greg must have noticed. He offers to give us a moment before we leave.

"Nonny," I choke out her name and lunge for a hug. She crumbles a little, and that only makes me sadder. We pull away and both wipe our eyes.

"We're a wreck." Nonny wipes her eyes and laughs. She seems much older, like she aged during the flight. "God has a plan, Hadley. You wait and see." I can't find my voice so I swallow the lump in my throat and nod my head. It's so strange to have such a somber moment in a playroom, surrounded by army men, race cars, and a Wii. I yawn, exhausted as the events of the day catch up with me.

###

Later that night, everything seems off and strange. My stomach is tight with thoughts of staying in a new bed, in a new room, at a new house, with a new family. Everything is foreign. It gets a bit chaotic during Patrick and Libby's bedtime. Baths, stories, this is all unfamiliar territory for me. I call to check in with Nonny during the hustle and bustle to make sure she's okay and, confession, because I don't know what to do with myself right now. I'm glad to hear she's settled in and well, but I wish I could tell her "goodnight" in person. Greg invited Nonny to church with us tomorrow, so at least I don't have to wait long to see her again. I wonder what it will be like for Nonny to see so many people she hasn't spoken to in almost seventeen years?

After we hang up, I check my missed texts and find one auto-generated message from Broadwater High School:

Msg from Broadwater HS:
Student: Edwards, Hadley
Work Study: Southern Salvage
Peer Mentor: Colton Sturgest
Respond Y to confirm, H for help.

Honestly, I don't know what any of that means. And there are four from Taylor:

I miss yooooooou! Have a safe flight & text when you get there. Is the grass for real blue? Post a pic and tag me on insta.

I heard a myth that it takes twice as long to pour a diet Coke in flight because the air pressure causes it to foam more. Ask your flight attendant and report back. You know you want to, nerd.

Dang. There goes a missed opportunity.

Hello? Are you ok? What's the fam like? How's Nonny? Hadley? HADLEY?

Here's an idea—want to facetime a double date this weekend? Zero threat the guy will get handsy. Whatyasay?

Ok, she's totally trying to get a reaction out of me. I text back:

Thx for ur texts. Super tired. I'll be sure we talk tomorrow. Luv you, friend.

Also, heck to the no on the facetime date. I can't believe she still tried to set me up from 600 miles away.

On second thought, yes I can.

I take my time to enjoy a hot shower. On the way back to my room, I pass by Patrick's door. I don't want to interrupt their routine, so I tiptoe past. I'm stopped dead in my tracks when I hear a small, sleepy voice ask, "Does this mean I have to share Daddy?" Whoa. My gut clenches like a giant fist just slugged it. Yeah, I'm a huge interruption.

CHAPTER 4

New Dog, Same Stinky Poo

»» ———————————— ««

Where am I? It takes me a minute to filter through my groggy confusion. I rub one eye and peel open the other, and what do you know, there's a four-year-old *thisclose* to my face. He darts out of my room.

"Mooooooommmmmmmmmmmyyyyyyyyy. Hadwey's awwwwwaaaaake!" The pitter-patter of tiny feet fades down the stairs. That'll wake anyone up.

"Want some?" Libby stands barefoot in the door, chewing on a piece of bacon. Sections of her strawberry-blonde hair are matted to the sides of her head, the rest frizzles out in wild disarray. She has on lavender jammies and the leg of one side of her bottoms twists sideways around her ankle.

Of course I want some, it's bacon. I smile and shake my head yes. "Can you give me a minute to grab some jammy pants and use the potty?"

Libby throws a hand to her hip, elbow out, all sassy. "I'm eight. You don't have to call it the potty." Well, alrighty. I'm impressed she had the restraint to hold back the eye roll.

I blink, because how does one respond to that? There's silence for half a beat, then Libby shrugs and sees herself out. I pull on some joggers, do-my-business (because "potty" is so not an eight-year-old thing), and follow my nose to breakfast.

Being the fifth wheel means Greg pulls a mismatched chair to the kitchen table to fit me in. It's awkward, sure, but Karie has made French toast and it smells amazing.

"I ate fouw pieces." Patrick holds up four tiny fingers, his grin full of pride. I congratulate him while Karie mumbles something about metabolism and grocery bills. I slide two buttered slices onto my plate and pour syrup over the top while chomping on a strip of bacon. A dash of powdered sugar completes.

"This is delicious. Thank you." Uncomfortable as I am in my role of intruder, it would be rude not to say anything. Silence says, "I'm disrespectful" and I don't want that.

"Thank you. Do you want to help clean up and then we can get ready for church? Libby can show you how. We need to leave around ten to pick your grandmother up on the way." Karie pushes in her seat and places her plate by the sink.

Tension I didn't realize I was holding in my shoulders dissipates—I'm surprised I'm being voluntold to do chores so soon, but oddly enough it makes me feel like I actually belong? I wash pans and load the dishwasher. Libby wipes down the table and puts ingredients away, which is handy since I have no idea where anything goes.

I cringe when I look in the mirror once I'm dressed for church. I don't have the clothes I packed for the movers, so my only respectable option is a pair of khaki shorts and a plain teal top. T-strap leather sandals will have to do. A knock sounds and Karie sticks her head in the partially opened door. She must notice my apprehension. "What's wrong?"

"Can I wear this to your church? I wouldn't wear this to a church picnic back home." I open my arms to show my ensemble.

"We go to a pretty casual church." Karie steps in and reveals capris and a white eyelet tunic top. Huh, maybe I won't embarrass the new 'rents. "If you want, you can borrow a necklace. That will polish off your look."

She leaves for a minute but it's Greg who returns, a simple floating pearl necklace in hand. "Um. Karie said you might want this?" He coughs uncomfortably and…is he blushing? He holds the necklace up and neither one of us is sure what to do next.

He clears his throat. "If you can hold your hair up, I'll fasten the clasp for you." He gestures for me to turn.

I lift my hair in my palms and he brings the chain over my head. The necklace settles around my collar and tickles where he closes the clasp. It's foreign and fatherly all at once.

###

When we get to church, I offer to help sign Patrick into the Kid's Kingdom room then walk with Libby to Children's Church. On my way to the sanctuary, I get turned around and have to ask for directions.

A giant bear of a man with a Fu Manchu and a toothpick hanging from his bottom lip takes a hard look at me and blinks. "Shoo wee, honey, you must be Jenny Edwards' girl. You're the spittin' image of your momma. Is she here? I haven't seen her in years."

You and me both, dude. Those words don't leave my lips, though there are some questions I'd like to ask him. Instead, I take a deep breath and exhale my apprehension. "Er, no sir. I'm here with … my grandmother. Can you point me to the sanctuary, please?"

"Sure, hon. I'm Mike, and this young man walkin' up is my nephew, Colton."

I shift my attention to Colton, and, in the wise and articulate words of Mike, *shoo wee,* he is gorgeous. Chestnut brown hair, textured and messy. Captivating gray-blue eyes. My mouth stops working and I can only produce the traditional lame-o greeting of "Hi" followed by what I'm sure is an intense blush, judging by the heat radiating from my cheeks.

"Colton, can you please show …" Mike looks at me as if he's expecting something.

"Oh, Hadley. I'm Hadley." Smooth. My middle name is "Awkward." I don't say that either.

"Can you please show Hadley to the sanctuary?"

Embarrassed to be such a burden, I'm unsure of how I should respond if he says no. He wouldn't, would he? Southern hospitality and all that.

"Sorry, Uncle Mike, I've got to take the snack to Children's Church before Mrs. Sue gets upset. Nice to meet you, Haley."

Hmmm. "Nice to meet" me. Was it, though? I glare at his retreating form. He didn't seem like the good Samaritan one might expect when a stranger needs an escort to a sanctuary. And my name isn't Haley.

Mike's lips purse and his eyebrows scrunch together. "Hadley, those snacks are some kind of important. Let me get you to your pew."

I spot Nonny and take my seat right beside her, smooshing myself in at the end. Her presence is like a faithful, familiar buoy in an uncharted sea of unfamiliarity. So many people stop to greet Nonny, expressing their surprise to see her. I could fill the offering plate if I were paid a dollar every time I heard "...It's been so long!" Nonny introduces me to so many people, all surprised to meet her granddaughter. Considering the countless curious stares, you'd think I was Jenny Edwards' clone.

"When your mother was younger, all the youth sat in the same place, there to the left." Nonny gestures a few rows closer to the front and sure enough, there are about twenty or so teens right around my age. They seem chatty and friendly, and I can't help but wonder if I'll fit in with the crowd. How many go to Broadwater High School? Guess I'll find out tomorrow. I take a deep breath and try to focus on the sermon.

###

That afternoon, I tear up during my Facetime with Taylor, which catches us both off guard.

"Spill, Hadley. What's wrong?" Taylor is perceptive, that's for sure.

"Um, my first day is tomorrow. I'm the newbie." My voice sounds pathetic.

Her voice bubbles with typical Taylor enthusiasm. "Exactly! You get a fresh start. And I know you, Hadley. I bet you've already memorized your schedule and mapped out the most efficient routes between classes. Amiright?"

"Stop it, I have not." I have.

"It's normal to be nervous. Heck, it would be weird if you weren't. But I'm always a text away. And remember, fresh start." The fresh start spiel would make sense if I needed a new beginning, but I ache to go back to Annapolis and my old friends.

Monday morning, I grab my backpack from Karie's backseat and try to shake my anxiety. She gives me a "go get 'em" wink before heading off to her office in the guidance counselors' suite. I weave through a swarm of students and enter the brick building through large double doors with columns on each side and find my way to the front office. The secretary directs me to a chair from which I watch my new classmates filter in and scatter to their lockers.

It's a short wait because only five minutes pass before a student council member arrives to give me a tour. A gorgeous brunette who could be the next Miss Teen America introduces herself.

"I'm Kyra," the model offers. Kyra's hair is impossibly shiny, like glass, and if she doesn't already, she should make YouTube tutorials on how to apply flawless make-up. This girl could have endorsements from a toothpaste company and facial wash. It's hard not to stare.

She picks at a piece of invisible lint on her dark wash jeans and smiles politely. Kyra's friendly, and although I get the impression her cordial demeanor is sincere, she also seems...disinterested? Distracted? Like, she's probably perfectly nice, but maybe I'm the hundredth tour she's given today and when she's finished, she can finally go do something fun.

Kyra gives me the typical run-of-mill tour, walking me from class to class and introducing each teacher. She shows me where to find the gym and cafeteria, explains which bathrooms are better than others, and adds a plug for student council, albeit not a very enthusiastic one. Finally, and with an exaggerated sigh, Krya deposits me back at the front office.

"I hope you have a wonderful day. Please let me know if I can be of help to you." Is she still talking to me? Her overly excited, obnoxious Barbie voice was absent during the tour. I get the impression her performance is for the benefit of the office staff. She excuses herself to go to her first period and I catch her smile slip, replaced with a pinched expression. Interesting. And Broadwater High School must be super-efficient, because for the second time today, I sit for only a few minutes when an elderly gentleman opens the door and smiles at me.

"Miss Edwards, I'm Mr. Howardson. Please do follow me to my classroom."

We leave the main office and I follow him down the Social Studies hall, all the way to a very empty room 116.

I help myself to a seat. Mr. Howardson sits in his ancient leather rolling chair and shuffles a stack of papers at his desk.

"Miss Hadley, it's a pleasure to finally meet you in person. I trust Kyra gave you a pleasant tour?"

"Yes sir, thank you." Nothing special, but nice enough. Basic American high school. As the Captain might have once said "Different dog. Same stinky poo."

"I know Kyra showed you to each of your classes, but I have a printed schedule for you anyway. And here is an agenda book." He places both at the end of his desk. "You'll also need to stop by the Library Media Center to pick up your Chromebook."

"Thank you." I swear I have a more extensive vocabulary, but this seems to be the only phrase I know today.

"I don't know if you are already aware that the completion of a student's senior year here at Broadwater High School requires a service project within the community. As your advisor and chair of the History Department, I've taken the liberty of placing you with Mr. Sturgest at Southern Salvage. A member of the staff will be your mentor and will assist you in completing your project." He places a manila folder with information on my growing stack.

I bite my lip as I fumble with the straps of my bag. I was *not* already aware. I should have paid more attention to that mystery text. Also, *salvage?*

"My real strengths are in math and science, Mr. Howardson. Are there any projects or mentors in those fields?" I'm fidgeting with a hangnail as I ask this, my apprehension over this potential placement causing me to yank skin off my pinky.

"I'm afraid not, Hadley. Your enrollment was a bit late and occurred after placements were made. Southern Salvage is a prized local establishment and, to be frank, you're lucky they were still available. If you go in with an open mind, you might actually enjoy working with antiques. Be sure to check your folder for all the information."

Holy cow, antiques? I sag back into my seat and force a smile for Mr. Howardson. Show me a teenager who says they enjoy antiques and I'll show you a liar. But I don't protest because something about his tone as he made that last statement said, "*This is final.*"

"Thank you, Mr. Howardson." I take the information and leave his classroom. The bell to signal the end of first period blasts out at a volume that can't possibly be healthy for one's auditory health, and students begin to trickle into the classroom. I shoulder my way through a sea of unfamiliar faces and try to remember which hallway hosts second-period calculus. Now, math, that's a subject I can wrap my head around. Math only has a wrong or right answer. No gray areas in calculus!

###

Most of the rest of my first day flies by in a blur. I have Honors English 3, AP U.S. History, Chemistry, and art *(art!)* as my last period elective. Taylor would be so proud. But you know what? I like art because I like the teacher, Mr. Moses, who I kid you not is Bob Ross reincarnated and may have actually gone to high school with his namesake, he's that old. I'm not crafty but staring at his curly waif makes me downright eager to paint mountains, lakes, and happy little trees. Although PE would have been helpful to keep me in shape for cross country, Bob Ross 2.0 might work. So, satisfied with my happy little scheduling accident, I take an open seat between two students and make small talk while starting our first assignment, a contour drawing.

"So, you're a senior, huh? Do you have a work-study yet?" Red curly hair to my right, whose name is Raven, seems friendly.

"I've been placed at a business called Southern Salvage. Know anything about it?"

She drops her pen at this revelation and leans across me to get the attention of my neighbor to my left. "Ashley!

Southern Salvage is accepting work study applicants again and Hadley here volunteered as tribute."

Well, that doesn't sound good.

My jaw goes slack and I grip my pencil harder. "Um, should I be nervous? What's with the *Hunger Games* analogy?" Seriously though.

Ashley's eyebrows rise. "Southern Salvage is all kinds of awesome, but the owner, Mr. Sturgest is...something." Unfortunately, she doesn't elaborate.

Raven gives a shiver. "He served in Vietnam and is legit terrifying. Scary stuff, no lie. Too much Agent Orange and all that. But his grandson? Eye candy."

"Total eye candy." They sigh collectively and bat their eyelashes. It seems both Raven and Ashley find his hotness to be legendary.

Raven continues. "Broadwater frickin' loves the whole BHS senior work-study thing. Eats it up! And it raises a truckload of money for the town trust. Mr. Sturgest used to accept students but stopped two or three years ago. Rumor has it he was too abrasive and the work study kids complained. I guess he got fed up or ran out of patience because he hasn't accepted one since. Even his grandson, Colton, had to intern somewhere else when he was a senior two years ago!"

I frown. Where have I heard that name before?

Raven taps her pencil on the guy in front of us and whispers, "The newbie's work-study is at Southern Salvage!"

He turns and his eyes get as big as saucers. "Do you like Norman Bates movies?"

I'm sorry, what?

When Mr. (Bob Ross) Moses circulates the room and makes it over to our row Raven decides to announce my fate to him as well. His raised eyebrows are not promising either. And that's how my last class ends.

So yeah, a *little* scared for my whole work-study experience. Why couldn't Broadwater have a Naval lab?

###

That evening, after a plate of meatloaf and mashed potatoes is set in front of me, Karie initiates conversation with the question, "What was the most interesting thing you learned at school?"

Libby is quick to jump in with the tale from science class, where, in a lesson about the solar system, her future husband (her words, no lie) Andrew was chosen by the teacher to volunteer as the sun. She was Mars and rotated like a boss. Patrick, not to go unnoticed, shared that his best friend Will ate two whole Uncrustables at lunch, and asks, "Why can't I pack a lunch?"

It seems it's my turn, and the table quiets as they await my response. This is worse than being called on in Mrs. Shelton's class.

"Um, well–" I bite at my lip and try to think of something, anything, but my insides are tangled in knots and I don't think it's Karie's cooking.

Greg clears his throat. "Let's give Hadley a pass tonight. First day at a new school and she isn't familiar with our dinner routine."

"Promise you'll go first tomorrow?" Libby sticks out an impressive puppy dog lip.

"Promise." I slump back in my chair, grateful.

Ah, tomorrow. What new worries will Tuesday bring?

CHAPTER 5

Blessed are the Homesick

»» ———————————— ««

Tuesday afternoon, I roll my shoulders back and fidget with the necklace Taylor gave me. I approach Southern Salvage and swallow my fear. Interestingly, the shop is housed inside the town's old fire department, which was recently replaced by a fancy, newer structure. A historical marker stands beside the sidewalk outside the storefront, welcoming me to the Broadwater Historic District, and boy is it ever historic! This part of Kentucky apparently hosted the Trail of Tears and at one time welcomed soldiers from both Union and Confederate troops during the Civil War. I'm sucked into the detailed writings of the marker when an older gentleman clears his throat. I look up, pleased to be greeted by a sincere and friendly smile.

"You must be Hadley, correct?"

"Yes sir." And since the Captain always stressed the importance of eye-contact when making a first impression, I stare straight into his soul and offer my best and firmest handshake.

"I'm Mr. Sturgest. Pleased to meet you." He doesn't appear stoic or intimidating, as my peers would have me believe. Quite the opposite. Mr. Sturgest opens the front door of the shop and offers to give me a tour of the place. He gestures toward the counter.

"See this here? This beast is a collection of antique metal lockers, turned on their sides and polished patina, topped with reclaimed barn wood. Pretty neat, huh?" The gleam in his eyes draws a smile out of me. I hope he doesn't realize he may as well be speaking Greek.

A huge, antique register, the kind with the giant brass numbers, sits atop the modified-locker-counter-thingy. The entire set-up is kind of awesome. The floor is sealed concrete throughout. If vintage nostalgia is your thing, Southern Salvage is the place to be.

First, Mr. Sturgest, or Charles, as he invites me to call him, takes me through the right half of the store. We pass through an entryway carved out of exposed brick and bordered by antiquated molding. Here, a hodgepodge of architectural elements creates an organized chaos. Stacks of reclaimed fireplace mantels, crates filled with hardware such as antique doorknobs, columns, light fixtures of all types (SO. MANY. LIGHTS.) even old window frames with bubble glass, and an entire room full of various sizes and styles of salvaged doors.

We circle around to the left of the store, where reclaimed and repurposed materials are given new life and are available to purchase from consignors true to the

Southern Salvage brand. An old upright piano has been turned on its side, gutted, and morphed into an amazing bookcase. He points out galvanized metal pipes that have been welded into amazing sculptures I wouldn't have thought possible if I hadn't seen them myself. And the reclaimed stained-glass windows that hang from the ceiling are breathtaking, as are their price tags. I get the impression Charles can read minds, because he looks at me with a curious expression.

"Sorry, it's just... I'm sixteen, sir. I could buy a car for that price." Just when I fear I've offended him by saying the wrong thing, he erupts with an epic belly laugh in response.

In the middle of the Southern Salvage warehouse is a custom design center of sorts named The Way Maker, where, Charles explains, patrons can commission pieces to be created from materials they've brought with them or purchased in house. It's there that I see him, the super friendly Samaritan from church.

Charles gestures. "Hadley, this is my nephew, Colton. Colton, Hadley."

Nephew? How many uncles can one kid have? I fix a friendly smile on my face, but Colton, who appears to be building something out of the parts from dismantled bourbon barrels, barely affords me a glance. I might be afraid of dating, but I'm not blind. Ashley and Raven weren't joking when they said Colton Sturgest is, *ahem*, easy on the eyes. He's tall, around six feet or more, and his dark hair is hanging in messy wafts from his baseball hat. The bill of his cap can't hide his blue eyes or full lips. I bite the inside of my cheek and force myself to look away.

"You'll be working closest with Colton, as he'll be the one to help you create the project required for your work-study. My dad, William, is Colton's grandfather and the owner of this place." Oh. Well. That explains things. This level of confusion might require an illustrated Sturgest family tree.

"Hi Hadley, nice to meet you." Colton offers a tight smile, then turns to my guide "Uncle Charles, can you see if Mike has picked up the stain for this headboard?"

"Absolutely. Let me finish up with Hadley and I'll get right to it." After Charles assures Colton he'll check on the stain, we continue our tour. Do other people ever suspect they might be invisible, or is it only me? Apparently, I didn't make a huge impression when we met *two days ago.*

From The Way Maker station, I follow Charles outside through the back and enter a courtyard. It looks like a junkyard, albeit a very well-organized one. Rusty clawfoot bathtubs, slabs of granite, cast-iron railings, stone planters, and stuff I don't even know the names of lay piled in orderly heaps. To say I'm overwhelmed is an understatement.

"Any idea what you might want to create for your project?"

"And suggestions?" I smile, to which he laughs.

"Afraid I'm fresh out, but I do wish you good luck." He opens the door for me and gestures for me to go ahead. "Why don't we head back inside and I'll introduce you to the scary Mr. Sturgest and you can get him to sign your paperwork?"

I chuckle at his candor and follow him to the office where I meet him, the man who looks astonishingly similar to the Captain. Tall, broad shoulders, and a neatly trimmed, stark white beard. I take a minute to gather myself, which I'm sure isn't the best first impression I could make, and close my gaping mouth.

"Have a seat, Miss Edwards." Of all the amazing items in this store, the shabby, dilapidated, brown and orange plaid couch he motions to is not one of them. I guess he can read eyebrows, because he presses his lips together in the tiniest of grins and says, "Old Faithful won't bite, she's quite comfy." Oh my word, they've named this monstrosity of a sofa. I take a seat on the dust mite mausoleum as Mr. Sturgest claims a high-back chair behind a giant desk. I listen as Mr. Sturgest basically repeats all that Mr. Howardson and Charles have already told me.

He crosses his arms over his broad chest and furrows his brow. "I haven't had an intern in a few years, Hadley. I hope I won't regret changing my mind."

Gulp. "I'm looking forward to interning here, sir. Thank you for the opportunity." I'll just interact with Mr. Sturgest the same way I would with the Captain. I can do this. And I'm going to repeat my personal pep-talk until I believe it myself. I'm not afraid of Old Man Sturgest anyway, I'm afraid of his cold-hearted, gorgeous grandson.

I take the long way "home," a word I use loosely because it certainly doesn't feel like home, and stop by Broadwater Assisted Living to visit with Nonny. I sign the guest book at the reception desk and shoot Karie and *Da*— nope, can't do it— *Greg* a text to let them know I'm here. Will I ever be able to call Greg "Dad?" It's too weird. You can't go without a father for almost seventeen years then flip a switch and refer to a stranger as "Dad." "Father" is too formal, and "Poppa" makes me sound like a smurf.

"Ma'am?" A lady at the desk looks at me expectantly; apparently I zoned out for a second.

I blink a few times. "Oh, yes. I'm here to visit with Dawna Edwards, please." I wrap my arms around my waist as a wave of uncertainty washes over me.

"Sure hon, right this way." The kind, elderly employee with bouffant hair who could very well be a resident herself, escorts me to the dining room, where I find my grandmother enjoying chocolate mousse at a table full of friends. It's like Queen Nonny is holding court. Terminal cancer has aged her since her diagnosis, but she seems much younger than most of the other residents. Time passes in weird ways, I guess.

"Excuse me, ladies, my beautiful Hadley has arrived!" Her face lights up when she introduces me, and I offer my best smile. It feels hollow. I'm so happy to see Nonny, but I hate the circumstances.

I follow her past a group of older men piecing together a jigsaw puzzle, straight to her apartment, Suite 215. I haven't been to her living space in a few days, and she's decorated it much like our home in Annapolis. The quilt that used to grace the back of our recliner rests on her couch. The same painting of the Annapolis waterfront hangs on her wall. I tear up, overwhelmed by the familiarity. It's all our same stuff, but outside of our home in Maryland, they look artificial and foreign.

"Give Nonny a hug, Hun." She wraps frail arms, once strong, around me. I'm scared to give her a proper hug in return. We sit and she adjusts her treatment port through her shirt.

"Are you okay, Nonny?" I want to know, but I'm afraid to find out.

"Of course, of course. The doctor is taking my port out tomorrow. I can't believe it—I've had this old thing for years and I'm finally getting rid of it!" She seems thrilled, but I know that means she's given up treatment. I swallow the lump in the back of my throat. The removal of that port means cancer wins, and defeat weighs heavily on my chest.

"What's botherin' you, sugar?" She asks this quietly, and I take a deep breath. Do I share my troubles or spare her?

"Do you know any Sturgests, Nonny? My work-study placement is with Southern Salvage, and their family owns the place." I wait.

"Oh yes, the work study. Everyone loves the senior project. Been around since my time."

"Wait, really? What was your project?" I lean forward, intrigued.

"Hmm yes, I taught dance to the senior citizens right here at Broadwater Assisted Living. I can still salsa with the best of them." She gives a slight shimmy and grins. "We had a recital at the end and charged admission. I raised $50 for the town trust. And in the late 1970's, that wasn't exactly chump change. Money went farther then."

I have a fun image of Nonny dancing in a peasant blouse and bell-bottoms, just like the one of her and the Captain that used to hang in our hallway back home.

Before my reverie turns to despair, I focus my attention back to Southern Salvage.

"So, you're not sure if you remember any Sturgests?" I hate that my voice sounds desperate.

"I know a few Sturgests. Was that Mike that helped you to our pew at church on Sunday? Heard he was married to a pediatrician. Believe it was Mrs. Patty's daughter, Lesley."

Nonny has the memory of an elephant. She continues. "Mike is the goofy brother. Charles has always been the quiet one, but very kind. One girl, their sister Lydia. I remember her as very kind-hearted. William, the dad, he was always a little of both. After Vietnam, he seemed a little more reserved. Reminds me a lot of your grandfather, come to think of it." Nonny takes a deep breath, and I notice her eyes look tired. Her face doesn't have its normal glow, and it seems I should go. I don't want to leave, but I can't stand thinking I'm tiring her out.

"I better go so I can help Karie with dinner." The words fly out of my mouth before I can talk myself into staying longer.

"Yes, Hun, you get on home. Come back, soon." I start to rise but I reach down to hug her before she can get up, hoping this helps her save some energy. I don't have the heart to tell Nonny I'm not going home. I'm going to the Kendall's house, and they're not the same thing.

###

I know Karie is going to ask me, "What's the most interesting thing you learned at school today." So, by the time dinner rolls around, I'm ready for my interrogation like I've prepped for the Spanish Inquisition. Last night I promised Libby I'd go first today, and in true eight-year-old fashion, she hasn't forgotten.

Cheetos, which are classified as chips–*they're not*– burn longer than Veggie Chips–*also not chips*–because they have a higher caloric content. This was the most interesting fact I learned at school today, thanks to my monotone Chemistry teacher, Mr. Wilson. He assigned me the chore of lighting a Cheeto on fire and, although this seemed like a waste of cheesy goodness to me, it helped me measure the "chip's" calories. This doesn't seem like a skill I'll need in the future since I don't plan to torch my steak anytime soon, but I'm told live-action chemistry can't hurt when I'm prepping for the SATs. Libby's response to my Cheetos story is, "Sounds like a waste of perfectly good Cheetos, if you ask me."

I smile. "I thought the same thing."

Our exchange makes me grin. We are definitely sisters from the same mister. We've got the same color hair, hers slightly darker and shorter. The style matches her spunk. Our eyes are the same shade of hazel, more green than brown. I steal a glance at her and I can practically see the wheels turning. She's thinking of something.

"Mother, father," she starts, and at such formal titles they share a nervous glance, "in the name of science, these brussels sprouts must be torched!"

CHAPTER 6

Pressing Matters

»» ———————————— ««

On Thursday I officially start my internship. It's a quick five blocks from the front steps of the Kendall house to the front door of Southern Salvage, so it only takes me about five leisurely minutes. I head around the back and step over a few quirky concrete gnomes on my way through the side door Charles showed me. The gnomes freak me out, all diminutive and mischievous looking. All except for the cute pink one in the corner that I decide to name Twinkles because she's adorable. Does the face that I'm naming inanimate objects mean I need to make some friends? Have I turned into Tom Hank's character from *Cast Away*, who befriended a volleyball he dubbed Wilson? Oh well. Tom Hanks is awesome, so Twinkles can be Twinkles and nobody has to know.

I walk through the front of the store with my most graceful swagger and head for the Waymaker Station–and crash right into a gigantic, uh, thing? "Grrrrr." I grab my leg and wonder why there're so many nerve endings in a shin. That's when I notice two pairs of gorgeous eyes staring at me. Colton and what appears to be his super-hot, petite girlfriend.

Grrrr indeed.

"Hey Hadley, glad you could make it. This is my cousin Franny. Franny, meet Hadley." Cousin. Phew. Why it's such a relief that his beautiful sidekick is actually kin, I don't care to think about.

"Nice to meet you, Franny." I offer a polite smile and receive a surprisingly firm handshake from someone so tiny. Small but mighty, I guess.

"Same, thanks. I'm going to check on the front counter and I'll see you guys later." She bounces on her toes as she walks off. I like her immediately. Colton goes back to staining the headboard he's been working on in silence.

A massive wooden machine lumbers across from him, cabinets and drawers with an enormous component that looks like a giant screw in the middle.

"Is this...a printing press?" I'm sure I sound super intelligent today. Honestly, I'm realizing one never knows what they might find in *Southern Salvage.*

Colton offers a heart-stopping smile and I spy a dimple. "Nice guess, Gutenberg."

"It's HUGE!" I sputter. "Where did that come from and what are you going to do with it?"

He stops staining and leans closer to the machine, and me, so I'm suddenly focused on my printing press education. "This is a Paul Shniedewend & Co Antique

Washington Style Printing Press from the 1800s. It was forgotten in the library basement at Centre College until a few months ago. They're remodeling the lower level of the building into some fancy-schmancy tech lab, and we got it for a steal." His enthusiasm is adorable.

"It's really cool." I tilt my head forward to admire the machine, fidgeting with the diecast types and meddling with the smooth cast iron letters. "Wait." I jerk my hands back to my chest. "Is it okay that I'm touching these?"

"Yeah, it's fine." Colton seems to swallow a laugh and continues. "The librarian told me Centre College purchased this press in 1908, right before the football team's historic win over Harvard College, 6-0. They used it to print over 500 copies of the student newspaper with 'C6HO' and posted them all over campus and the town. They still have an original one framed on the wall at Mug Masters."

"Cool." I'm surprised to find that conversations with Colton seem easy. Maybe I already have a friend. I'll have to get Twinkle's opinions on being part of a trio. "Can I print something?"

"Knock yourself out. Except don't really knock yourself out. Might be hard to cheat death with a thing that weighs 1,800 pounds. Be careful." Eyebrows drawn together, he actually looks pretty concerned as he says this.

"Meh, I've cheated before. Ain't no thang." I mean, does cheating death while jaywalking count? I can't believe he trusts me enough to mess with this giant machine, but I get started before he changes his mind. I line the doohickey with the letters to form my favorite verse, Proverbs 3:5-6. It takes longer than I would have expected. I roll the ink across the letters and turn to ask Colton to help me with the heavy lever. "Hey, would you mind–"

"I can't help you with your project today so don't worry about staying until 5. You can leave now." Or maybe not. Colton seems a little frosty all of a sudden. Arms are crossed over his chest and his lips are turned down in a tight frown, his expression hard. I'm usually great at discerning people's emotions, but he won't even look at me.

I open my mouth to ask about his sudden change in mood but think better of it. Instead, I start to clean up the mess I've made when he clips "No, I'll get it."

"Fine. Whatever." Dismissed yet again, I grab my bag wondering what the heck happened and give a curt nod to Twinkles on my way out.

Since I've got some free time, I take the long way back and stop by Broadwater Assisted Living. I sign in and head down the hall to find the door to suite 215 wide open, with Nonny enjoying an afternoon snack.

"Hadley!" Nonny's face lights up. "You have to try one of these delightful scones. A coffee shop down the street dropped them off for the residents this afternoon." She gestures to a bag with a Mug Masters logo on the front and slides it my way. I take the seat beside her and peek inside. It smells delicious, but my stomach is still tight from being rejected by my mentor.

"You got your appetite back." A little tension eases from my shoulders. It seems like Nonny is getting stronger, the opposite of what I was bracing myself for.

Nonny puts a hand to her heart then lowers it. "Yes. Today I have an appetite. You remember Dr. Stein said that sometimes happens when cancer patients stop chemo, right? He said when the toxins from the medicine leave one's body they can sometimes get better before the cancer makes them feel worse."

I don't remember that, and I don't want to. The tightness in my shoulders comes back with a vengeance. I nod to Nonny and grieve the loss of ignorance.

"I don't think my mentor, Colton, likes me very much." Where this came from, I don't know, but I'm grateful for the change in subject.

"Colton Sturgest? Well, I'm sure he likes you fine, hon. You're usually more worried a boy *will* like you." She chuckles to herself, but I remain silent, my lips pinched in a thin line.

61

"I thought we were making progress since we first met at church, but at my internship he's always hot or cold. Today was like nuclear winter."

"Something to pray about. God is still good." This is, by far, the most Nonny thing to say in all the universe. If I've heard it once, I've heard it one thousand times. I will not allow myself to groan in response.

We spend the rest of our time picking at the scones and enjoying Nonny's soap opera. Then, I mosey back to the Kendall house. Home, but not quite.

###

Apparently, Broadwater High School has a different schedule every other Friday to accommodate clubs. Naturally, I'm lost and have no idea where I'm supposed to be or when.

I spot a familiar face. "Raven! I'm the sole member of Club Lost. Can you help me find somewhere to go? Like math club?"

"Isn't that for nerds?" Her slow smile builds.

With conviction, I tell Raven, "Math club is for dedicated mathletes like myself."

Raven blinks. "Oh my gosh, you *are* a nerd. Anyway, sis, you could go to math club *next* Friday. It isn't on today's club schedule rotation."

"Oh." Well, that's deflating. My shoulders fall from my ears. "Where are you headed?"

"Art club. It's math club's cooler, free-spirited cousin. Want to come?" Raven raises an eyebrow.

"Sure" is what comes out of my treacherous mouth, even though I do not want to go to art club. I also don't want to spend Club Day in a bathroom stall reading a book by myself. Again. I finished five pages of Macbeth for AP English during extended class change yesterday, so at least my self-inflicted solitary confinement was productive.

No shock here, but the art club meets in the art room, so I find myself sitting in my usual seat between Raven and Ashley. Creature of habit, I guess. We pick up the presorted square papers and follow Mr. Moses instructions to create different origami pieces. My crumpled swan looks like it needs to be euthanized.

"Started your project yet? How is Southern Salvage?" Ashley presses in a fold on a beautiful paper butterfly. I'm impressed. And a little jealous.

"Well, Mike is hilarious and Charles seems pretty friendly. Mr. Sturgest isn't half as scary as I thought he would be. I guess the cold-hearted part skipped a generation and a concentrated dose went straight to Colton."

"Wait, what?" Raven stares, her confusion genuine.

"Colton Sturgest is not a Hadley fan." I deadpan.

Her brows pinch together as she considers what I've said. "But Colton has always been so warm and friendly. He's, like, super nice."

"As in, he-might-be-a-closet-serial-killer-fake-nice?" Why do I have a bad feeling he is as nice as they say he is, but his problem is specifically with me?

"No. Just…nice." Raven says. They both stare at me now, their expressions hard to read.

"Huh," is all I can say.

"Maybe you caught him on a bad day," Raven offers.

I don't think so. It has to be something else, and it might drive me crazy trying to figure out exactly what.

###

"So, what were you thinking about for your project? Remind me of the requirements and I can help you brainstorm," Colton says. I guess the nice version of Jekyll and Hyde is back.

"Well, it has to be a community service project that benefits me academically and Broadwater's Town Trust monetarily. Whatever project I—excuse me, *we*—create will be auctioned off at the fall festival in November. After that, I will give a culminating report on the project in December." I open the folder Mr. Howardson gave me and pull out the document with the project specifics. "We don't have a budget. We're not required to spend money to complete the project, but we're not penalized for purchasing supplies. However, we cannot cause our mentoring business to incur expenses. The auction item(s) submitted must be a students' original work and the student must recognize that the object will be given up/submitted for auction. Oh! There is an extra credit notice!" I rub my hands together, giddy.

Colton rolls his eyes at my enthusiasm and shakes his head.

I continue. "The auction item that earns the highest winning bid will be featured in the *Broadwater Beacon Magazine* along with an article about their mentor." Now, I won't say I'm drooling, but I'm pretty excited. I'm not just a nerd, I'm a *competitive* nerd!

"Yeah, calm down," Colton says, and my enthusiasm dies a little. "Why don't you take a lap around the store and the alleyway to brainstorm a list of potential ideas?" He hands me one of those weird automotive grease pencils—the ones you have to peel off the outside to get to the marking part—and a pad of paper. I'm pretty sure I've been brushed off *again*. I'm a big girl, I can deal. It's just that I wish I knew *why* he disliked me. I clench my teeth and, with what I hope isn't obvious reluctance, take the materials he's offered and walk away.

###

All this worry about why a person I barely know practically loathes me has caused some serious anxiety. You know what quiets an anxious soul? Prayer. You know what else does? Stress eating, but that's not helpful. It's running. Running is helpful, and who should walk into the room as I'm lacing up my shoes? Libby.

"*NO WAY.*" The reverence in her whisper surprises me. "Are you going *running?*" Confused, I stop lacing mid-tie and look at her, nodding slowly as I await her explanation.

"Did you know that 3rd grade is the first year students can go out for cross-country? Tryouts are in, like, two weeks and I'm s'posed to run an *ENTIRE* mile *WITHOUT* stopping." Her giant eyes glow as she talks. This kid has a flair for the dramatics.

"Welllllllll, I happened to be on the cross-country and track teams in Maryland. I can help you train for your tryouts."

"Shut up." Libby slaps a hand over her mouth and races to add, "That was the nice kind of 'shut up,' like, 'oh em gee, yes I would love that' kind of shut up. Not the get-in-trouble kind." Her flushed cheeks tell me she's more than a little panicked.

"Relax, I knew what you meant. Do you have a good pair of shoes, some shorts, and a running bra?"

"A WUT?" There is some major eight-year-old side-eye 'tude coming from her face.

"Ok, forget the B-R-A. Can you go get some socks and shoes?"

She runs to her closet before I can even finish my sentence and has her Nike's double knotted in five seconds flat.

We leave a note on the kitchen island for Karie and I take my phone with me just in case. We stretch in the driveway, and I help her map out a course. Libby's so excited she's bouncing from foot to foot and I get a little tickled.

"You ready?" And I kid you not, bam, she's off. "Easy killer, you're setting a wicked pace!"

She. Is. Rolling. She makes it to the end of the street at break-neck speed when I finally catch up to her.

"How far have we gone?" she gasps.

"Um, about three tenths of a mile?"

"*What?*" She doesn't seem to believe it and promptly stops, taking a seat right in the middle of the sidewalk.

"Whoa, whoa, whoa. We can't quit that easily. You've got this, Libs." The nickname earns me more of her serious stink eye, so I correct myself. "Libby." She smiles. Kind of. I mean, she's panting so she *tries* to smile.

"Why don't we catch our breath and try it again? We'll set a steady pace and focus on finishing. Then, as we get better, we'll try to run portions of our route a little faster each time. Does that sound like a plan?"

"I'm listening…" And bless her heart she really is, frozen in her spot with her eyes trained on me.

"Do you want to play a game while we run? Taylor and I sometimes play games to distract ourselves."

"It would be nice to concentrate on something other than my exploding lungs." Libby's voice drips with sarcasm. Yeah, she's definitely Taylor's mini-me.

"Ok, let's take turns naming something from—I don't know, you pick the category—and we have to say them in alphabetical order. So, if we did animals, I might say 'Aardvark,' and you would go next. You might say—"

"Baboon!"

"Yes! Baboon…" We start to jog and I focus on keeping a steady pace.

"Chipmunk!"

"Dolphin."

"Elephant…"

We get all the way to letter *T* by the time we finish the course we mapped out. We circle back to the front of the house and head in for dinner.

"MOM! Libby took me running and listen, I think this is going to be my thing, I really do."

"Call the International Olympics Committee," I quip.

You know what else distracts from stress? A spunky insta-sis, that's what.

And I am distracted, until I notice Karie's pursed lips and realize something isn't right.

"You forgot Patrick, Hadley." Her arms cross as she says it and my stomach sinks.

"I... did?" I did? Where did Libby sneak off to? I glance around and she is nowhere.

"Yes. You were supposed to wait at the door for the preschool van. They can't leave a child at home alone." Her hands are actually shaking and I think I might get sick. I close my eyes and take a deep breath in an effort to calm myself.

"I am so sorry." This is bad. Big bad. "I swear I didn't know."

"That's enough, Hadley. I know you're not used to being responsible for younger siblings, but you've got to realize Patrick is four. Four! You're not the center of attention here." She may as well have slapped me with that little comment. She doesn't notice my discomfort and I try to hush my anxiety while she carries on.

"Thankfully, Mrs. Warsaw was home and went to church with the driver. Patrick waited at her house until I got home." At my sigh of relief, she raises her voice and says, "She's seventy-eight!" Yikes.

Greg suddenly appears and interrupts. "Hi. I, um, well…it seems like I might have forgotten to tell Hadley about Patrick's preschool transportation plan? Maybe?"

Karie's posture goes rigid, her eyes wide. She blows out a huge breath and swallows. "Hadley, please allow me to–"

But I don't wait to hear the rest. Like Libby, I check out. I can't even remember walking back to my room, but I close the door and sink to the floor, burying my head in my hands.

###

Saturday morning, after my customary greeting to my BFF, Twinkles, I head to the back of Southern Salvage and sort glass insulators for Mr. Sturgest while humming quietly to Lauren Daigle's 'Light of the World' as it plays on the speaker. Colton does his best to ignore me. Considering I have more than two months to work with him, I'm trying to balance warming him up to me while simultaneously not being annoying. I hum more softly so he doesn't find me obnoxious, but stop to ask, "What are these, anyway?"

Colton offers a long explanation about how "Insulators are those glass things you see on the tops of old telephone poles. They used to insulate the electrical wires so electricity wouldn't leak into the pole and earth and... stuff." The scientist in me gestures for him to continue, he seems pretty into it...

"Conduction of electricity requires electrons to move a potential charge through the material... " Heaven help me, I'm trying to listen...blah blah blah, "—to conduct electricity. So basically, glass doesn't conduct electricity." He sounds a bit like Bill Nye's apprentice as he says all this.

I'm pretty sure my chin has dropped open, so I quickly correct my slack jaw.

"Brilliant TED Talk, sir. So, what does Southern Salvage use these for? There must be three or four dozen here."

"Mostly tea light holders or sometimes retro pendants," he answers. "One Christmas Uncle Mike made an entire insulator Christmas tree. That was kind of awesome." He smiles at the memory and his face lights up. I try not to drool. "It was actually pretty big; he ended up giving it to the UK Children's Hospital in Lexington. You can still go see it every year from November until the New Year. It's a big hit with the kids."

Ok, that is pretty cool. I'm admiring the way the light reflects through the insulator's glass and humming along to more Lauren Daigle when an idea strikes.

"What if I made a light?" I blurt out. Colton looks at me quizzically, so I continue. "For my project? Not out of insulators, but I could use some type of salvaged material—because that's history—and the electrical component would include circuits and stuff—that's science—and there would be a little math in there for kicks, then BAM, I've got myself a perfectly acceptable, cross-curricular project! What do you think?"

"What's wrong with using insulators? We have so many my dad would probably pay you to take them."

My heart drums with excitement and my brain goes into overdrive as neurons fire with an avalanche of ideas. "Not original enough. I'm still working on that part."

CHAPTER 7

Lightbulb!

»» ———————— ««

Saturdays are busy at Southern Salvage. I squeeze through the side entrance and strain to catch a glimpse of Twinkles. This place is a maze of customers and merch, but I stay occupied doing whatever the Sturgest family needs. I've sought out Colton a few times since I got here an hour ago, and it's clear he's avoiding me. Massive surprise. I still haven't decided on a project and Twinkles is pretty tight-lipped, per usual.

Instead, I help set up a chalk paint display with Mike and Franny. I'm distracted by his bright pink tee that reads, "Don't laugh, this is your girlfriend's shirt." Wide-eyed, I point to the caption and whisper to Franny, "Is he serious right now?"

She rolls her eyes, "Is he *ever* serious?"

"What?" he asks, straight-faced, "This is my wife's favorite one!" And then he winks, so I guess he must be joking. Right?

I close my gaping mouth as Colton strides up, appearing from out of nowhere. Finally. He pushes a giant cart of snacks and drinks towards the staff office and the sight of them makes my stomach growl. Unfortunately, it's nowhere near lunchtime.

"Hey Franny, hey Mike. Hadley, you need to narrow down a project, the sooner the better."

Well, hello to you too, gorgeous jerk. I purse my lips together to avoid sticking my tongue out. Also, he looks mad. Those normally clear eyes of his are dark with anger. He probably wants to get started so he can get finished and be rid of me because, apparently, I'm a parasite.

"What ideas did you come up with the other day?" He crosses his arms over his chest, impatient and annoyed.

All three pairs of eyes focus on me, as if the weight of the world hinges on my decision.

"Oh, um, well." Crap. "I thought I could use the printing press to replicate old Broadwater posters. Give them a vintage feel and sell those?" Their glazed eyes appear unimpressed. "Or I could use the screen printer to make cool Broadwater shirts." I look to Mike for approval, since he seems to be the screen-printing T-shirt guru around here, but his blank expression tells me that's a no-go, too. I list off half a dozen lame ideas I found on Pinterest, and they go over like a pregnant pole-vaulter.

Mike grabs one of Coke bottles from Colton's cart and uses the string tied bottle opener to pop the lid. The fizz is quiet, but loud enough to mercifully break the awkward silence. A thought strikes me and the birth of an idea tingles in my mind.

Mike catches me concentrating on the shine of the galvanized metal cart. "Now don't go trying to check your reflection. You girls are always tryin' to re-apply your lip gloss."

At this, I not-so-accidentally nudge the cart just hard enough to graze his shin.

"Oof! Typical woman driver." He shakes his head.

"He's kidding." Colton mumbles, rubbing his hand on his forehead. "It's his schtick. Tries to pretend he's a total masochist. He's not."

Mike's a little too good at his so-called "schtick."

"He loves Aunt Lesley, don't let him fool you." Franny rolls her eyes again.

Mike takes another giant swig from his soda bottle and slams it down on the cart. "Mmmm, yes, she's the light of my life." He clutches his chest and makes doe-y eyes.

"That's it!" I burst out. They stare at me with confusion. "I can create an epic hanging light fixture out of soda bottles for my project. Like a crystal Coke chandelier."

"Wouldn't that take a ton of bottles?" Colton looks to Mike for confirmation. "And you'd have to somehow cut each bottle, assuming you can even get enough. And figure out a way to insert and light a bulb in every single one."

"And connect them to a fixture," Franny interjects.

"And wire it properly." Mike this time.

"But… it can be done, right?"

"Well, yeah, sure, but it's going to be hard. And time consuming. And the projects aren't supposed to be expensive, but I don't see how you can avoid that."

I'm not afraid of hard work. Why so much doubt? "Ye of little faith, Colton. I know you've never met my Nonny, but she's taught me all kinds of awesomeness. 'With God all things are possible.' That's Matthew 19:26. And 'God is able to do immeasurably more than all we ask or imagine' is from Ephesians 3:20. And everybody knows 'I can do all things through Christ who strengthens me' from Philippians 4:13. We got this, amiright?" I look to each of them for support. I am on a roll and my excitement has me bouncing on my toes.

"Preach, sister!" Franny wears a huge grin.

Colton's eyes grow wide at my unexpected enthusiasm. His expression melts from surprised admiration to something like confusion and I can't read it well at all. He opens his mouth, but nothing comes out. But then Mike, bless him, studies me for a moment. He finishes off the last of his soda, hands me the bottle, and says "You can start with this one." He squeezes my shoulder and nods in approval of my ambitious plan, right before he walks off with the cart.

Mike might be the only guy that approves of my "bright" idea. Colton spends the remaining two hours of my shift vacillating between experiencing a silent existential crisis or trying to persuade me into choosing a project on a smaller scale. At one point he suggests Mod-Podging coasters. Um, no. Does he genuinely think my idea is too ambitious or does he just realize he'll have to spend more time with me and he's trying to avoid that at all costs? At noon, I head to the staff room to grab my bag, but as I head for the way out, he steps through the door, stands tall, and lays it all on the line.

"If you're really going to create some giant soda chandelier, you have to bring me a detailed plan of how you expect to complete this project. That's what I do when I'm working in the Waymaker Station, and I expect the same from you. I want to-scale measurements, cost estimates, construction details, everything. Bring that Tuesday or I will pick a new project for you."

Well. "Yes… sir?" I mean, he's only two years older than me, but he is my mentor. The lines are a little too blurry for him to boss me around like this. But I respect authority, and I am desperate to make this light fixture. It's like the idea picked me and now I need to make it.

"Hey, Colton?" I blurt out as he starts to walk away.

He freezes, half turning to face me. "Yeah?"

"You mean 'we.' We're going to create an amazing giant soda chandelier."

"Sure, whatever." Why does he have to look so attractive when he patronizes me?

###

As is routine, I head to Broadwater Assisted Living on my way back. Nonny looks like she isn't feeling her best today. I can tell she's been waiting for me, but she doesn't get up when I walk in. She has a weak smile on her pale face, but she's smiling none the less. She pats the couch next to her for me to sit, then hands me a card and says, "Happy early birthday! I have to give you this now or my plan won't work."

I blink back my surprise. What in the world? I tear open the purple envelope and gasp. Tucked inside a cute card is a flight itinerary with Taylor's name. She's flying to Lexington next week for my birthday! My seventeenth falls on the extended Labor Day Weekend so I get three full days and two nights with my bestie. Maybe this day isn't so terrible after all.

"The Kendalls are in on the secret, so they're happy to have Taylor stay with you. But there's one caveat, Hadley."

Nonny looks sheepish. "You'll have to figure out transportation to and from the airport."

Oh. Dang it.

###

Nonny didn't feel well enough for church this morning and I can't stop thinking about how she never likes to miss it. My stomach aches thinking about the memory of her empty seat in the pew and I beg to be excused from lunch. I'd rather be alone right now, but my siblings didn't get the memo that Sunday is a day of rest.

"Whatcha workin' on?" Goldfish crumbs tumble to my beige bedroom carpet as Libby and Patrick watch me scribble on the paper at my desk. I'm Facetiming Taylor while I calculate bottle costs and estimate wiring length. I should be writing my report for history that's due tomorrow, but I guess I didn't realize this would be so overwhelming. It's a great distraction from my helpless concern, though.

"Just trying to figure out how to make a light out of old soda bottles." I tap my pencil against my notebook, staring at nothing and hoping words and figures will appear like magic.

"Well, how's it going?" More crumbs fall on the floor.

"We'll see, I guess." I offer a shrug. "Want to say 'hi' to Taylor?"

Libby climbs into my lap and they wave to each other through the screen. Libby shares how we've been running every other day and reports on her times and distances. Taylor *oohs* and *ahhhhs* at all the right moments. I stare in admiration at her natural way with Libby–Taylor's had way more experience being a big sister than me, and it shows. We agree to run together when Taylor comes to visit before we sign off… and right after Taylor points out that Patrick is coloring my comforter with markers. Yeah, I definitely need help in the big-sister area.

###

Tuesday I'm on the verge of running late (and by running, I mean literally—I'm still as car-less as ever), and as I rush through the store front, Mike whistles as he glances at his watch. Such an exaggerated gesture. "Pound-sign cutting it close, Miss Punctuality."

"Hashtag-close-only-counts-in-hand-grenades-and-horseshoes!" I offer, and hurry to the back to put my things down in the staff room. "Hey! I'm sorry. I know I'm not late, but I was afraid I would be and I ran in here like a mad woman and–*OH!*" The last thing I expect to see is Colton standing by the desk, glowering at Kyra, her shoulders slumped as she sits on Old Faithful. He's pinching the bridge of his nose, and his jaw is clenched.

He looks up abruptly. "Hi Hadley, no worries. I'm glad you're here." Well, a pig flew by, too. "Kyra was just leaving."

"Think about what I said. Please?" Kyra clears her throat and turns to leave, her eyes red like she's been crying. She brushes past me and offers a tight-lipped smile, but there's deep sadness in her expression. What have I interrupted?

The silence is thick so I fiddle with the zipper of my bag while I consider how I might disappear or fall into the floor.

"Sorry about that." Colton's voice is so quiet at first, I think I imagined it. He runs his fingers through his dark hair and turns back to the office desk.

"Nothing to be sorry for." Gulp.

"Did you bring the write-up I asked for Saturday?"

"Sure did." Grateful for a distraction, I grab my notebook from my backpack and spread the papers out on the table.

He mumbles to himself as he reads my plans, dragging a finger down the paper as he does. "Let's see...five rings...suspended by chains...fifty-two bottles on ring one...forty bottles on ring two...twenty-eight...twenty-one...eight bottles on ring five."

Colton continues to consider my work, head tilted to the side, arms now crossed. Finally, he declares, "This... this is good." Another pig flies by and my chin drops.

"Wait, really?" I ask, and my treacherous cheeks warm up. I hate that my blush makes me look like a tomato. I should be embarrassed that his praise garners such a reaction, but he's been dangling the carrot a little too far since I started this internship.

"Really. Listen, Uncle Charles is sending me and Franny to Lexington Friday night to pick up some old barnwood and Mike thinks you should go too. They've got an old Coke bottling factory, and you might be able to get some bottles. Do you think your mom and dad would let you go?"

"I can ask Karie and Greg. Um, is there any chance this trip could include an impromptu detour to the airport?" The desperation in my voice sounds pathetic.

"Uhhhh... what's at the airport?"

I can't even hide my smile. "Taylor."

He's taking so long to answer and I *know* he's going to say no.

"I don't see why not. The bottle factory is like a mile from the airport."

I barely contain a squeal and Colton looks at me through squinted eyes. "You're not going to hug me, are you?"

Well, that sobers me right up. "Colton. I. Do. Not. Hug." If he values his arms, he won't try to, either. For some reason, my response earns me a lovely chuckle.

Friday seems infinitely far away. This might be a slow week.

CHAPTER 8

A Cut Above

»» ———————————— ««

I never would have guessed Karie and Greg would agree to let me go to Lexington Friday–I'm guessing they're grateful they don't have to worry about transporting Taylor from the airport. It's Wednesday, so I also get to see Nonny for dinner before church.

After school, I find Greg in the backyard mowing while Karie tends to a small garden. Patrick and Libby are running laps between the two. They look overwhelmed. "Greg, do you care if I take Libby and Patrick for a walk to Mug Masters? I'm worried Nonny's losing weight and I know she loves their scones. I thought maybe we could go for a fun afternoon treat and pick up a few."

"Please take these yahoos somewhere and bless you for offering." He wipes the sweat from his brow, and, despite his sarcasm, his light tone suggests he's kidding. He adores his kids. "Grab a twenty from my wallet and keep the change."

"Yes sir. Thank you."

"Kids, take a walk to Mug Masters with your sister." His command is followed by squeals of delight. "But not too many sweets before dinner!"

It takes longer to walk with a four-year-old. I almost melt when he reaches for my hand with his tiny little fingers. He hops, skips, and jumps the entire way, which is both adorable and incredibly inefficient.

We finally make it and we're greeted by that unique coffee shop smell as we open the door. I don't even like coffee, but the aroma is delicious. I've never been inside Mug Masters, and I love it the moment we step through the door. The atmosphere is warm and inviting. Besides the customary tables and chairs, there are also community bookshelves, cozy couches, low lighting, and leather chairs surrounding a giant coffee table with board games. The dark hardwood floors remind me of the ones from home in Annapolis. On one brick wall, I spot the framed C6H0 article Colton described on my first day as an intern. I have to confess, it is pretty cool.

As we saunter up to the counter, I'm awed by the giant cinnamon rolls bigger than our faces, chocolate croissants, and every kind of muffin imaginable. Patrick smooshes his nose against the glass case to admire the most beautiful cookies I've ever seen. Libby might actually be drooling.

"Pwease, Hadwey. Can I pwease have a cookie?" Patrick has puppy dog eyes and my resistance slips.

"Hi Hadley." Kyra's wearing a Mug Master's apron like it's a prom dress. How does she do that? "I know Mrs. Kendall sometimes lets her kids share a cookie or a muffin." She smiles. Libby, however, is not smiling. Disgruntled that Kyra would commit such treacherous betrayal and spill the only-half-a-cookie secret, she crosses her arms and sticks out her bottom lip.

"Sorry, kid. Your mom is my favorite counselor at school. I don't want to get on her bad side." Kyra winks at Libby and her lip retracts. A little, anyway.

"I'll take one cookie–the biggest one you can find–and four scones to go, please."

"What flavor scones? We have blueberry, blueberry-lemon, cranberry-orange, and vanilla."

"Oh, I don't know? Do you know what kind Broadwater Assisted Living usually orders? These are for my Nonny." I start to panic and rub at the back of my neck with my Patrick-free hand.

"I'm sorry, I don't." Based on her sympathetic smile, Kyra can tell I'm anxious about getting this order right.

"No worries. How about one of each?" I press my lips together. I wish I could remember Nonny's favorite.

Kyra rings up our total and packages the scones in a paper bag. She cuts the giant cookie in half and offers one to each child. Based on their greedy eyes, I'd say she now ranks right up there with Santa Claus. She hesitates, then asks, "So, you're interning at Southern Salvage?"

"Oh, um, yes. It's… interesting."

"I bet." Well, that's cryptic.

I'm not sure how to respond, so I tell her about my project. "I'm hoping to create a chandelier out of old Coke bottles, but those things don't grow on trees, so…"

"Like these?" Kyra points to a fridge with soda bottles, parfaits, and an assortment of teas and juices.

"Yes! Just like those. Do you have any extra?" I try to keep my face blank to avoid seeming overly hopeful, but free bottles would be huge.

"Uh, definitely. Let me check recycling." Kyra comes back with a large Mug Masters catering box filled with about a dozen empty bottles. "You'll have to clean them," she makes a face, "but you're welcome to them. And Hadley…" She hesitates.

"Hm?"

"Can you let Colton know I was happy to give them to you?"

I don't know her ulterior motive in this, but her secret is my gain. "Sure," I shrug. "And thank you so much." She smiles, lets out what I can only assume is a breath of relief, and returns to her register to help a waiting patron.

At school on Thursday, I'm required to update Mr. Howardson on my project.

"My Hadley, this is ambitious." Is that doubt in his voice? I really hope he isn't joining team Debbie Doubters.

"I thought that was a good thing? Something ambitious can raise more money, right?" *Please don't kill my project.*

"Oh, I absolutely believe you can do it, Miss Edwards. My only concern would be the expenses. How might you keep your costs to a minimum?

"I plan to pay in cryptocurrency, Pepsi Points, and Monopoly Money." Just kidding. That's what I want to say, but in my infinite wisdom I shrug and offer a sheepish grin. "I'll have to cross that bridge when I get there, I suppose."

"You'll need to *get there* sooner rather than later if you're planning on finishing this chandelier by the fall festival."

Oof. "Yes sir."

That afternoon, I take my dozen freshly scrubbed Coke bottles and add them to the one Mike gave me. Thirteen. Not so bad. Take that, Howardson.

I spend the first thirty minutes of my time at Southern Salvage watching YouTube videos on how to cut glass using something called the string method. Finally, Colton calls me over to the Waymaker Station where he has boiling water on a hot plate, a bucket of ice, gloves, sandpaper, and a scoring tool already set up. Forget the string method and YouTube, Colton knows what's up.

"Ready?" He asks. "I can show you how to cut your bottle and you can practice on some random glass I found around the shop."

"*Bottles.*" I offer a satisfied grin at my use of the plural. "Kyra gave these to me when I stopped by Mug Masters for Nonny's scones yesterday. She asked me to pass that tidbit of info your way." I watch his face with caution to read his reaction. Completely blank expression. Mental note: Do not play poker with Colton Sturgest.

Alrighty then. I make a motion to the tools and he launches into mentor mode, giving instructions at such a fast pace I struggle to keep up. But he's an excellent teacher and pauses often to check that I understand. He stares into my eyes each time he clarifies something, and it is unnerving. He's also a hands-on type of teacher. Colton touches my hand to show how to score the glass and an electric zing passes through my fingers. Am I the only one who felt that? He seems completely unaffected, yet I'm totally distracted by his strong hands and his muscular forearm that is distinctly male. He'll have to give this same lesson all over again.

I fumble the scoring tool twice, but he stays as calm and patient as ever. When he finally seems confident in my ability to do simple tasks a monkey could master more quickly than me, he excuses himself to help Franny and encourages me to practice. At least he won't notice my blushing face from across the store. He was one-hundred percent professional, so why is my stomach in knots?

Between trying my best to not relive my glass cutting lesson and hoping I'll have to anyway, I barely slept a wink last night. Fortunately, I'm not the least bit tired. It's finally Friday, the day of Taylor's visit, and I am giddy for three whole days with my bestie.

School isn't so bad, club day and all, but five p.m. took its sweet time coming. I make my way to Southern Salvage and load into the Southern Salvage Truck with Franny and Colton, who sit up front while I take my seat in the extended cab in the back. I'm sure they're having a riveting conversation, but I can't stop mentally planning my time with Taylor.

After we pick up the reclaimed barn wood, we head to the bottle factory. We're greeted by Mr. Pepper, the Sturgests' contact at Bluegrass Bottling. I explain my project and my low-cost predicament.

"Hmmmm. Have you heard of our Reduce Reuse Recycle sustainability initiative?"

"No, sir." I can't even say that three times fast.

"Reduce, Reuse, Recycle is our solution to promote sustainability and our commitment to our community and our environment. We recycle all bottles returned to this facility, but we also have unused bottles with tiny defects. It sounds like you could repurpose those for your light. Are you familiar with how social media endorsements work?"

"Like, where people get paid per post and number of subscribers?"

He nods and runs his hands over his graying beard. "Something like that. Why don't we make a deal? As you complete your project, you post pictures on your social media accounts and tag Bluegrass Bottling as you do. Post two to three times a week for the next five weeks to highlight your project and one photo of the final product. You can have 150 bottles for the posts, ten bottles per post, fifteen posts in total."

"That's… awesome! But–"

"*But?*" Colton's blue eyes look like they're about to pop out of his gorgeous head.

"But I'm not allowed to have social media." Womp, womp.

They all blink at me like I've grown a second head.

I shrink into myself and shrug. "What? My grandmother raised me. Nonny thinks phones are only for calls and Snapchat is the spawn of Satan."

Bless their gracious hearts, no one rolls their eyes at me. Colton stares at the parking lot. I don't mention how much I appreciate that a lack of social media lets me fly under the radar of public scrutiny.

"We could make the posts on our Southern Salvage accounts," Franny suggests. "We've got a healthy number of followers on all the major social media platforms. Could Hadley still have the endorsement deal?"

Mr. Pepper considers this. "Yes, I don't see why that wouldn't work. Let me grab some paperwork and get your signatures. I'll have those bottles packed for you shortly."

I help Colton and Mr. Pepper load up the truck with what seems like an insane number of bottles, and the magnitude of the project hits me. Self-doubt creeps in, and Colton's "told you so" smirk only feeds my insecurity.

With a half-hour to kill before we're scheduled to pick up Taylor, we head to the airport Chick-fil-A. I can't wait to tell Libby we counted a record twelve "My pleasures."

CHAPTER 9

Reunited and it Feels so Good

»» ———————————— ««

I am so grateful Colton and Franny conceded to a pit stop at Lexington's Bluegrass Airport to pick up Taylor. I can't get over the beautiful views. Franny has a theory that the deep green fields are so green they look almost blue, hence the name Bluegrass. At any event, "Horse-country" is not a misnomer. Muscled colts and fillies run or graze in the open fields. We drive through the pickup lane and Taylor stands on the curb, watching the cars pass. She's changed her hair back to blonde with a purple ombre. Of course, she's beautiful. My heart squeezes in my chest as it hits me how much I've missed her. We've barely pulled to a stop, but I practically jump out of the car and tackle her in a bear hug.

"Whoa—what happened to Side-Hug-Hadley?"

I gaze downward and cringe–is it too much to hope Colton and Franny didn't hear that? They'll never let me live it down.

I make the introductions, and when Taylor meets Colton, her eyes grow bright and she gives me a look like I've been hiding something. As he puts Taylor's bags in the back, she pokes me in the ribs and her eyes beg me for an explanation. Franny smirks in mild amusement as she follows along.

"He is gorgeous, Hadley," she whispers under her breath as she playfully nudges me in the side.

"He can't stand me, Taylor," I hiss through my closed teeth and the fake smile plastered on my face.

Franny's eyebrows squish together as she starts to interject, but before she can say anything, Colton closes the tailgate and walks back around. Her reaction makes my stomach flutter and I'd pay to know what she was about to say.

"Ladies." He gestures to the truck, and we pile back in and buckle up. Then I notice the gift-wrapped box Taylor's kept separate from the rest of her bags.

"Taylor!" Pleased, she offers the gift, making a show of handing it over in a royal manner.

"My birthday isn't until tomorrow." My heart is racing, and I can't imagine what this could be.

"Right, but I suggest you open this particular gift now." She's insistent, so I tear into the package and, heaven help me, I want to cry.

"Puckett's! You brought me Puckett's!" I reverently lift the two quarts of creamy custard out of the dry ice cooler.

"Oh my gosh, oh my gosh, oh my gosh, thank you so much for such an awesome, thoughtful gift." A second spontaneous side-hug is in order, surprising both of us.

"Figures. Is food like your love language?" Franny jokes.

"Yes," Taylor and I say in unison. We look at each other, then burst out laughing. Then burst into laughter again when Colton and Franny exchange glances.

We spend the first ten or fifteen minutes of the ride catching up on Annapolis news, then I share information about my internship at Southern Salvage and all things Broadwater High School. I remember too late bringing up anything related to BHS Tigers is a bad idea. I forgot my friend's affinity for playing cupid.

"Ohmygosh, Hadley! What about homecoming? That's got to be coming up, right? You *have* to go to homecoming. Have no fear. Your dating guru has arrived." Groan. "Tell me about your prospects. Has anyone expressed interest? Is there anyone *you're* interested in?" She wiggles her eyebrows in a suggestive way.

"Taylor," I warn.

"What? You don't have a throng of boyfriends lined up?" she quips. Then, to my horror, she turns to the front seat and declares, "Hadley's such a man-eater, that one."

"Hilarious. Can we change the subject?" I beg, squirming in my seat, my face hot.

Colton clears his throat and I catch him taking a peek in the rearview mirror. His frigid eyes send a wicked shiver right through me, at least until he snaps them back to the road.

"Didn't you have a few boyfriends before you moved from Maryland? Like, at the same time?" Colton has an edge to his voice and his question comes from out of left field.

Taylor barks out a laugh in response. "Um, what boyfriend would that be?" She clearly missed the tension in Colton's voice.

She leans into the passenger seat with a conspiratorial grin. "Are y'all serious? Hadley has *never* had a boyfriend. Heck, Hadley rarely goes on a second date if I can even convince her to go on a first. She's terrified of dating and boys in general. How have you not noticed this?"

Colton's head flinches as his eyes snap back to the rearview mirror again. I try to avoid eye contact, but I can feel my cheeks flame. I stifle a groan and can't imagine what's going through his and Franny's minds right now. It would be nice if I could shrink into a ball, roll out the car door, and be smooshed flat on I-75 South.

But of course, Taylor isn't done. "Don't think I haven't done my part to cure her of this self-diagnosed allergy to boys by dragging her on a million double dates."

"Mostly against my will…" I mumble. The blistering heat moves to my ears until I'm sure they're as fire-engine red as my face.

"Wait, are you serious?" Franny looks so dumbfounded, I almost laugh. "Did you know that, Colton?" He raises his brows and looks like he wants to answer, but nothing comes out of his mouth.

"Why does it bother *you* so much that it doesn't bother *me* to be single? Just because I'm single doesn't mean I'm not whole. If you go to Puckett's and buy a single cheeseburger, don't you still get a *whole* friggin' burger?" I sweep a look over all of them.

There is an awkward silence as the car goes quiet at my miniature outburst, then they all break out in a fit of laughter.

I slump back into my seat. "Sorry," I say sheepishly.

Then their giggle fest starts all over again.

###

It's not until Colton drops me and Taylor off at my house that I can breathe at a normal rate again. Something changed or shifted in the car, and I can't quite figure out what. It wouldn't surprise me if Colton liked Taylor.

Everyone likes Taylor. Must be it. It doesn't matter. She lives quite far away and has a very devoted boyfriend. Not that he'll actually talk to me to find any of that out. But why does his possible-crush bother me?

I'm nervous to introduce Taylor to my insta-fam, but Karie has brownies waiting for us. She grabs Taylor for a hug, which doesn't faze her quite like it did me. I'm pleased to introduce Libby and Patrick, but I'm still hesitant to introduce my dad by anything other than Mr. Kendall. Awkward is not a pleasant experience. Taylor quickly takes to both Libby and Patrick, which makes sense since she has younger siblings. She's a natural. Even Patrick's brownie crumbs spilling into her lap doesn't faze her. Ew.

"So, Libby, how do you like having an insta-sis?" Only Taylor could ask this with so much sincerity.

Libby blushes. "When mommy told me she was going to have a baby, I wished for a sister." She grins at the memory. "But I love Bubby," she adds quickly.

"Of course you do, and I bet you're a great big sis. Now you also get to be a great little sis." And just like that, Taylor has won Libby over. "You know, I have a sister and there's nothing like it. You can ask each other for advice, borrow clothes–ooh, Hadley can drive you places! She loves the movies and—"

"Don't think the new family budgeted for their surprise teenager to get a car, Taylor," I interrupt, matter-of-fact tone in mind. Didn't mean to interrupt them, but don't want to give Libby false hope about any potential taxi services. I sneak a glance at the Kendalls, certain I've offended them, but they appear as chill as ever.

"Right. Well, I happen to know that Hadley is a great secret keeper, too. So, there's that!"

"And she's helping me get ready for my cross-country meet," Libby beams.

"I can help you too. I even brought my running shoes and sports bras." Libby snorts and I subtly shake my head no.

"'Bra' is like a four-letter word around these parts," I whisper to Taylor.

###

Saturday we "train" with Libby for her big cross-country meet. This time, we play the alphabet game with desserts, so we're starving by the end of our run. We wash up and get fancy, because of course, Taylor and Libby have that in common too. I'm forced to exchange my comfy denim shorts, Hey Dudes, and a faded T-shirt for a skirt (!), strappy sandals, and a teal top. Because that's normal. Our alphabet game had us salivating since the middle of mile two, and Karie suggests we walk Taylor to enjoy some of the local fare, her treat. Because of Taylor's coffee addiction, we walk down to Mug Masters, Karie's twenty-dollar bill in hand. What is it about coffee shops that make them smell so awesome? I take a deep breath and savor the aroma.

We wait in a lengthy but steady line and when we reach the counter, Kyra is our barista again.

Taylor steps behind Libby so she can stand in the front. "You first, Libby."

"May I please have a tall Zebra with no expresso?"

"Isn't that just expensive chocolate milk?" Sure sounds like a four-dollar small cup of expensive chocolate milk to me.

"To each their own," says the eight-year-old.

"Touché." Four-dollar small cup of overpriced chocolate milk it is.

Taylor's turn. "I'll take a triple, venti, half-sweet, non-fat, caramel macchiato, please."

"Are you even speaking English?" I mutter. Taylor smiles.

"And for you?" Kyra looks right at me.

"Well... I don't like coffee, and I should calm down with the sweet iced tea. What's your most popular non-coffee, non-sweet tea drink?"

Kyra thinks for a minute, and I'm touched because she seems to consider my question. "I think you'd like a nice chai. Want to try one iced? If you don't like it, I'll replace it with something else."

"Sure." And *boy* is Kyra right. This might be my new life juice. "You 'barista' like a boss," I tell her.

She looks at me funny.

I smile sheepishly. "I made it a verb, it's cool." We leave Mug Masters and head down to show Taylor Southern Salvage.

As soon as we arrive, I can tell Taylor's impressed. Why this gives me a sense of relief I can't explain. She tips her head back to take in the splendor that is Southern Salvage. She moves carefully throughout the store, showing reverence to all the amazing items they have for sale. I give her the grand tour, walking through the massive store and basking in all its glory. Taylor stops by a vintage chair reupholstered in dark pink velvet.

"That. Looks. Awesome," she says. And it does. I walk her past the Waymaker Station to see the beginnings of my chandelier. "So, show me this project you're working on, woman."

I point to the hodgepodge pile of coke bottles, masking tape, wires, and tools. "Behold!"

Taylor seems underwhelmed. I show her how Colton taught me to cut the bottles and wire them properly. She watches me work and then her face brightens with an "Ah ha!" moment.

"You know, you could use the same wire cutters I use when I make jewelry." She shows me how to manipulate the wires and work them around the bottle tops. Libby toys with a few of the other tools while Taylor helps me to officially solder on the first three bottles. We're irrationally proud of ourselves.

###

That night, Taylor and I sit on the floor in my room, painting our toes and discussing her visit. We have ONE day left and we're bound and determined to make the most of it. We've already planned a post-run Sunday breakfast repeat of Karie's smorgasbord pancake buffet, then we'll head to Mug Masters for a last chai and whatever tongue-twister espresso drink Taylor wants.

Taylor stretches her long legs out and examines her freshly painted pink toes. "Puckett's isn't the same without you, Hadley."

I know that's her not-sappy way of saying she'll miss me, but I'm not ready for premature goodbyes. "Your visit has been a nice break from all this kid stuff."

Movement at my door catches my eye. Taylor and I see Libby at the same time, and when she frowns, she bolts from the bedroom.

I sit upright and freeze. "Taylor! You have siblings … what should I do? Pretend it didn't happen? Go now? Give her five minutes?"

Taylor moves closer and offers a small smile. "Being a sister is tough stuff sometimes, isn't it? First, deep breath. Second, I don't know Libby well, but she seems like an awesome kid. Go check on her, it couldn't hurt."

With cotton balls stuffed between wet toes, I hobble across the hall and knock quietly.

"Go away!" The sound of her sniffles tear at my insides. They sound like me starting to panic.

"I'd rather talk if that's alright with you?"

"*NO!*"

And great, here comes Karie with a load of laundry. "What's going on?"

In my selfishness, my first thought is: "Puh-lease do not have crazy momma bear claws!" I have a severe, self-diagnosed allergy to confrontation and do NOT want to get on my stepmom's bad side. Assuming she has one.

"I think I hurt Libby's feelings. Any advice, wise counselor?" I chew my lip. I'm sure I look as pathetic as I sound.

"Oh." She sets her laundry basket down. "I'll get the candy bowl."

Okay. I eat my stress too because it's delicious, but I wasn't expecting the trained psychologist to suggest it as a coping mechanism for her eight-year-old. "What? It couldn't hurt…" And Karie walks back to the kitchen.

Taylor is standing with me by the time Karie returns and knocks again.

"Go away!" Sigh.

"Libby Kendall, please open the door." I've never heard this mom-voice before and something about Karie's tone makes me want to live right. I ease the door open and find Libby seated at her desk, arms crossed, bottom lip out. We all pile in and Karie serves as a surprisingly unbiased mediator. She asks objective questions like "What happened?" and deals out the candy like a Vegas casino worker. Where was this mom when I "forgot" Patrick?

"Hadley and Taylor think they're too big and too cool to play with me." Libby's chin starts to quiver, and I close my eyes, suddenly overwhelmed with dread.

I love spending time with Libby, I just meant I could do without Barbies or diaper cream, but I doubt I can explain that to an eight-year-old.

Karie responds, "Well, sweetheart, it's important to remember that you're eight, albeit a very mature eight.

Hadley and Taylor are over twice your age. As far as I can tell, both young ladies love hanging out with you, but they're afraid they're boring you. They want to sip chia while you play with your slime kit, for example."

I don't think Libby is one hundred percent sold on Karie's counsel yet. Her little eyebrows furrow.

"You know what else?" Karie tilts her head thoughtfully. "You've had four whole years to master the whole sister gig, and Hadley is pretty new to the world of siblings. Try to remember she might need some help adjusting."

I. Love. Karie. #respect.

Libby nods her head, then walks over and hugs me. "I'm sorry, sis." I rest my chin on top of her head and squeeze my eyes shut, thankful for her show of grace.

Sunday morning, we enjoy the luxury of sleeping in, until Libby dive bombs my awesome bed to announce waffles for breakfast. If she weren't so cute and waffles weren't involved, that would not have gone well for her safety. Taylor, not quite the morning person I am, isn't enticed until Libby mentions bacon. We haul tail to the kitchen to discover not just fresh waffles, but an entire buffet, nay smorgasbord, of toppings. Karie doesn't mess around with Sunday breakfasts, but when guests are involved, it's no holds barred. There are M&M's, pecans, four different flavors of syrup, a container of peanut butter, sprinkles, Nutella, and stuff I've never even heard of. And bacon. Lots of bacon.

"Pace yourself," I hear Taylor whisper to herself.

So, we do. We enjoy a leisurely breakfast, then Taylor and I take our sweet time upstairs (we're "a little" uncomfortable from overeating). We take showers and get dressed in our Sunday best.

After church, Taylor and I enter Broadwater Assisted Living and I sign the visitors' log. It's lunch time, and most of the residents sit at their assigned tables. Taylor and I pull up a chair to wait for Nonny. When she's wheeled in, Taylor looks down at her lap and I stiffen. Nonny's never needed a wheelchair before. The sight of it takes my breath away.

"I didn't know she was this bad," Taylor whispers. I'm glad I warned her about Nonny's declining health in the car beforehand.

Nonny's caretaker parks her chair at the table, greets us with a smile, and excuses herself while Nonny unrolls her napkin and places it delicately in her lap. She smiles at Taylor.

"Oh sweetheart! What a treat to see your face. How are you, dear?" They make small talk as we wait for our food and I fidget with the artificial place setting of silk autumn leaves and fake pumpkins. We're served corned beef and cabbage, baked potatoes, spinach, a roll, and for dessert, tapioca fruit pudding. Nonny doesn't eat much, and I try not to let it worry me, but then again Taylor and I don't eat much either because, well … it's corned beef and cabbage. But they have sweet tea and I insist Taylor take a sip. I try not to scoff when she chokes a sip down and declares it "liquid diabetes." Nonny laughs and it is music to my ears. Leave it to Taylor to tell Nonny about my reluctance to attend homecoming.

"Oh, but what about that lovely Colton fellow, dear? He was so polite and quite handsome." Not Nonny too. My treacherous best friend grins.

###

My stomach is in knots as the end of Taylor's visit approaches. She rolls her suitcase into Southern Salvage and takes a seat to admire a giant rack of vintage clothes when Peter Staton from second period Algebra struts in. He waves to me and greets Taylor and Franny with a nod before heading to the room of doors.

Taylor looks at me with raised eyebrows and a goofy grin. She eyes Franny with a mischievous grin, and I know this cannot be good. Taylor hops up and we wander further around the store, stopping for Taylor to peruse some of the jewelry. I tell her to look as long as she'd like, and I slip off to check on my light fixture.

I find Colton cleaning up from working on the headboard when I hear the chime of the front door and notice Peter as he walks out. Taylor and Franny sneak up behind me like stealth ninjas. I shriek, then jerk my hands to cover my mouth, embarrassed by my outburst.

"We gave Peter your number," Taylor informs me. "He's going to pick you up Friday at seven. You're going to go to dinner and then the game. You're welcome." She and Franny fist bump.

My jaw drops and my frustration causes a slight tremor in my voice. "Franny! I hope you paid Judas there her thirty pieces of silver when you threw me under the bus. Do not collaborate with her. She needs no help."

They laugh hysterically, as if I've said all this in good humor (I didn't) but they're both caught up giggling at this like it's a silly joke, so I force myself to laugh along. Dating is not a joke; dating is a nightmare. My laughter fades much sooner than theirs does, and when I look up and make eye contact with Colton, I notice he isn't laughing at all. I break eye contact and rub at my forearms, suddenly self-conscious.

We have to head to the airport in half an hour, but Taylor is totally impressed with a consignor's upcycled jewelry display. She zeroes in on necklaces made from bottle caps, bracelets made from various metals, and especially rings made from silverware. I'm grateful for the change in conversation.

"Hadley, this is so you! Try this on…" She slips a particularly beautiful ring onto my finger and we both admire it.

That's when I notice Mr. Sturgest has decided *now* would be a convenient time to meet Taylor, because *of course he does.* I try to slip the ring off, but it won't budge.

"Little tight," I whisper through clenched teeth, and that's an understatement. I take a deep breath to try to calm the panic, but I swear a siren blares in my brain. Taylor must have ESP because she's quick to realize why I'm freaked out and acts fast.

"Isn't this ring gorgeous?" She shoves my hand in Mr. Sturgest's face.

He offers a tight-lipped smile. "You must be Taylor. Nice to meet you. I hope you've enjoyed visiting Broadwater and please let me know if you need any help."

It isn't until he walks off that I'm able to exhale. I can barely control the tears that threaten to spill over.

Taylor is quick in her attempt to calm my nerves. "Hey, no biggie! Just a tight ring."

"It isn't just the ring that doesn't *fit* around here, Tay." I wipe my tears with my palms and glance at the Waymaker Station. Franny and Colton wear matching "deer-in-the-headlight" expressions, but quickly busy themselves to avoid further awkwardness.

"Hadley, you got this. I'm sorry for shocking you with the whole Peter date thing, but I have a feeling you'll thank me later." She sounds so confident, I'm tempted to believe her.

CHAPTER 10

#SmittenKitten

»» ———————————— ««

"You ladies ready?" Colton has his hands in his pockets like he isn't sure what to do with them. He reaches for Taylor's suitcase, and I grab her carry on, our hands brushing. That mysterious electric current tingles where we touched. I shake it off and we head to the car. I hate goodbyes, and I'm putting this one off for as long as possible. Taylor tries to keep up the small talk during the drive, but I'm at a loss for what to add to the conversation. And why does the drive back feel so much shorter than the ride from the airport?

Colton parks the truck and we trudge as far as we can until we reach airport security. He hands Taylor her carry-on but lingers by the exit while I hug Taylor goodbye. In typical Taylor fashion, she ignores my misty eyes and leans in to whisper, "I love you. I'm praying for you and we both know God's got this. You're Hadley Edwards and you're amazing." Ugh. More water leaks from my eyes. I offer her a rare Hadley bearhug and then, she's off.

I wait at the security check until I can't see her anymore and slide a finger underneath each eye to clear away errant mascara. Colton is standing in the distance and I don't want to terrify him with a pathetic racoon face. I turn and he nods, maintaining eye contact while I walk back to him. Normally this might freak me out, but his stare is somehow comforting. My chest is tight. He gives me a light pat on the back and opens the door for me, leading me into the brisk outdoors. The wind whips at my hair so I duck my face against the cold, strands flying in disarray. We don't say much as we get back on the highway. Then, Colton makes a surprise turn into Starbucks, and I narrow my eyes at him. What is he up to? He gives me a small half-grin. When it's our turn at the drive-through he orders two iced chai teas and a couple of chocolate croissants.

"It's not Mug Masters, but... my treat. Franny told me your favorites."

Is he blushing?

This is so kind and unexpected—I'm afraid if I speak my voice will break, but I manage to smile and mumble my thanks. He either doesn't notice how emotional I am or pretends not to. I appreciate it either way. We enjoy our treats in companionable silence while I wonder about this new side of Colton.

Just as he's about to turn onto my street, I decide I'd rather see Nonny than fake a cheerful disposition toward my siblings. I don't have it in me.

"Wait. Do you mind dropping me off at Broadwater Assisted Living instead? I kind of want to spend some time with Nonny." I bite my bottom lip, hoping it will distract my eyes and more water won't sneak its way out.

"Yeah, sure." He switches his blinker and makes a left instead, pulling into the parking lot in no time. "Are you okay, Hadley? I'm happy to come in with you."

I may actually tear up all over again.

Who *is* this Colton? "No, but I appreciate the offer." I swallow the lump in my throat.

"Tell Nonny hi for me. I'll see you tomorrow."

"Yeah, see you tomorrow." I watch his truck as he drives off, completely perplexed by his change in demeanor. I don't hate it, though.

I find Nonny asleep in her La-Z-Boy, so not quite the visit I was hoping for. I pull a knitted Afghan off the back of her sofa and place it across her lap. I kiss her forehead and scribble a note on her notepad, writing "I love you, Nonny." I see myself out, clicking her door closed softly behind me.

###

Tuesday during art, Raven reaches over my desk and draws a tiny smiley face on my sketchpad. I look over, surprised.

"Seems like you need it. You're super quiet today. Mr. Sturgest suck the joy out of your life yet?" She's serious as she whispers, but her question gets a smile out of me.

"Not hardly. I kind of like it if I'm being honest. And Colton has been… sweet to me lately, which is new. And weird." I trail off as I consider his changed attitude toward me. I like Raven, but I don't know her well enough to open up about how much I miss Taylor or how worried I am about Nonny.

"You know, Colton really is a good guy. He had a tough time after Kyra cheated. Epic breakup, that one." Her voice goes quiet as she seems to mentally replay the awful split.

Hold up. Let me pull my jaw up off the floor before a gnat or something settles in.

"Kyra. Cheated. On Colton?" I blink and try my best to process the thoughts swirling in my head.

"Girl, how did you not know that? They dated for like two years." She's staring at me, wide-eyed, her curly red hair bouncing as she shakes her head.

"I had no idea." Colton obviously never confided in me, and Kyra always seems so nice.

I have difficulty concentrating the remainder of the day, which isn't ideal since I have a quiz tomorrow. Before

I can study, I'm off to Southern Salvage to work on a gigantic chandelier and post it all over social media.

I set up at the Waymaker Station, scoring one bottle after another. The technique Taylor showed me is great, but there are so many to cut, so I know this is going to get tedious fast.

"Hey Franny, can you grab your phone? Hadley should post something for Bluegrass Bottling soon." Colton lifts a box of bottles like it isn't full of heavy glass, setting it next to me with ease. My heart does a little flip. If he catches me checking out his biceps, I might actually pray for spontaneous combustion. But I'm quick to avert my eyes so I don't get caught.

"Almost ready." Franny is concentrating on something with her phone while I carefully place a scored bottle into the boiling water. Colton reaches over my shoulder to adjust the temperature on the hot plate and grazes my arm.

I will not swoon. I will *not* swoon. I will inhale, though, because he smells like boyfriend material. Earthy with a touch of mint. Fir needles, maybe? With a hint of Tide laundry detergent.

Oh my goodness, snap out of it.

I shake my head to regain my concentration, then use the tongs to move the bottle from the boiling water to the ice water. And then…

I hear the iPhone shutter sound. I definitely wasn't looking when Franny snapped that pic, but that must not matter because she's got a huge grin on her face.

"Epic." She gives us a thumbs-up and starts announcing hashtags, including #BluegrassBottlers, #BHSIntership and #SouthernSalvage. I quit counting after five hashtags, but Franny is on a roll. Colton shrugs and I continue scoring bottles. One more down, too many to count to go. I sneak a peek as Colton walks away to help a customer. It's difficult to think about much when he's near, but the room feels a little emptier when he's not in it. I can't help but wonder what Kyra was thinking. Girl needs a #lobotamy.

###

"Hey, Franny." I greet my friend with my signature side-hug, which I'm sure she recognizes as a true sign of endearment since Taylor outed my PDA aversion last weekend. We're meeting at Mug Masters to study for a calculus test before my routine Wednesday night Nonny visit and church. To be honest, math is my superpower, and I don't need to study much, but I am happy to hang out with my friend, so I keep my skills on the down low. We claim a table near the back where we won't be bothered, sit our study books down, and head to the counter to order. No surprise, Kyra is our barista.

She greets us with a stiff smile. "Franny, Haley." *Haley?* Is she being rude on purpose, or just pretending? She's called me by my name dozens of times. Franny does an amazing job of ignoring her jab and purchases a white hot chocolate.

I step up to the counter. "Hi, Krya. I'd like a Grande iced-chai te—"

"I'm guessing you'd like that chai 'skinny' right?" Kyra blinks at me, waiting for my response with narrow eyes and an annoyed smirk.

"W-what? What does 'skinny' mean?" I'm so confused.

"You know, 'skinny.' Made with skim milk to save calories." She gives me a slow once over.

Well, that was unexpected. Helloooo catty!

I blink. "Whole milk, please, and add a couple of pumps of vanilla syrup for kicks." I lay the exact change on the counter, skip the tip, and walk back to my seat hoping she doesn't spit in my drink. *What on earth?* And *dang it—* I forgot to order the chocolate croissants.

"Yeah…she definitely saw the post." Franny grits out from a fake, plastered-on smile as I take my seat in the chair across from her.

"What post?" Is there enough oxygen getting to my brain?

"The one from yesterday? I took a picture of you and Colton at the Waymaker Station and posted it to all of Southern Salvage's social media accounts." She pulls out her phone and shows me.

In the picture, my eyes are focused on the bottle I'm carefully gripping with the tongs, while Colton stands close to me, leaning over my shoulder and focused very much on... me. His gaze is fixed on my face, mouth open with the slightest smile, shoulders completely relaxed. His blue eyes shine. He's ridiculously handsome, as always. Even a blind person could see that.

He appears enamored—with me.

"Kind of looks like my cousin might be one smitten kitten." She smirks and takes a sip of her drink.

"No. No way." I squirm in my seat. Suddenly lightheaded, I shake my head. "You must have some kind of crazy filter on your phone or something..." I stop when Franny straightens in her seat, signaling our server delivering my drink. The cup is clearly short a few ounces, but at least it seems to be absent of spit.

"Are you ready yet?" Libby bursts into the bathroom while I brush my teeth, wearing full running clothes and clearly eager to go for our run. I've been walking on eggshells since the "kid stuff" comment, so I'm as anxious as she is.

"One sec…" Where did I put my hair band?

"Are you ready now?"

"Geez, kid. I'm almost ready, but you might appreciate it if I put on more deodorant first." Always a good idea.

Her face scrunches in disgust. "Puberty sounds like a real chore if you ask me."

That catches me off guard. "Good grief, how old are you?"

"Eight, but if you keep taking your sweet time, I'll be nine before we ever go on this run."

"Touché. And touchy. I'm as ready as I'll ever be. Sometimes when Taylor and I train, we run farther than the race we've got coming up to build up endurance, and, you know, confidence. How about we try for, say, one and a quarter mile?"

Her eyes narrow in suspicion, but she agrees. We head outside to stretch. As we prepare to start, she exclaims, "We can do 'Alphabet Desserts' today! Angel food cake!" And she's off. We make it all the way to *v* before we finish.

When we walk back through the front door, all giddy with our runner's high, I come crashing back to earth real quick. Karie sits on the bench in the foyer–the one where no one ever sits—her face pale and her hands clasped in her lap. I already know she's going to tell me something's happened to Nonny.

"Why don't you go clean up Libby, then help me set the table? Mommy needs to talk to Hadley."

CHAPTER 11

Colton Sees the Light

»» ———————————— ««

- *Residents at Broadwater Assisted Living must be able to walk, or have the ability to use a cane, walker or wheelchair independently.*

- *Residents requiring the attention of more than one staff member are recommended for care at a nursing home facility.*

Broadwater Assisted Living Bylaws

Karie, bless her heart, tries her best to explain the whole mess, but all I register is that Nonny needs to move from the assisted living facility to a nursing home. Which means A) Nonny is getting worse *fast* and B) I won't be able to make my routine visits on the way home anymore. I wish her weak, cancer-ridden body was as strong as her spirit and mind.

I also wish my eyes weren't so puffy from crying about it all night so I didn't have to explain it over and over again at school on Thursday. One more "I'm fine" and I will be one hundred percent *not* fine. I walk through most of the day on autopilot. Fortunately, I remember to congratulate Franny on her A+ quiz grade in calculus, but I ignore my lunch.

At least Raven manages to hide any pity during art. "Gonna get some caffeine or a cold compress to get those puffy eyes under control? You gotta big date tomorrow tonight."

Ugh. Does everyone know about Taylor and Franny's scheme? I've barely even talked to Peter.

She leans in and whispers, "Want to talk about it?"

I don't but I am so, so grateful she asked. I smile and nod my head no, willing the tears not to spill.

She offers a small smile and bumps my knee. "No problem. But seriously, get some of that sweet tea you're always going on about and some Advil or something and pull yourself together, woman." Bless her pseudo-abrasive self. She gives my shoulder a squeeze before she walks off at the dismissal bell.

After school, I offer a half-hearted wave to Twinkles on my way into Southern Salvage, but even her pink overall skirt doesn't seem as vibrant as usual. That afternoon, I work like a robot on my light fixture–I can't even remember how many bottles I've cut. They sit in a growing collection on the floor next to me.

"Hadley?" Colton waves a hand in front of my face.

I blink. "Sorry. Zoned out for a second."

"More like ten minutes. Everything ok?" He raises his eyebrows while he rolls up his sleeves, ready to help with the bottles.

I flush, then open my mouth and close it again, uncertain how much I'm ready and willing to share. He leans back against the counter of our station and stares at me.

"It's nothing." My voice is quiet.

He thumps the toe of his shoe against mine. "It's something. Spill."

I swallow. "Nonny isn't doing so hot. She has to move to Morningside Nursing Home this weekend."

"The one across town?" he asks.

"That's the one." I sigh, my chest heavy.

He nods and goes quiet for a minute. "Sorry, Hadley. I bet that's hard." Warmth washes through me as I process his sympathy.

We work in companionable silence, the quiet broken up by the occasional customer passing by and the clinking of glass.

"You ever driven down Gose Pike?" His sudden and unexpected question rips through the hushed workflow.

I lift a brow. "You mean in my Maserati?"

"Right, no car." He rubs the back of his neck and smiles. "You up for a ride?"

"Like, right now? Won't we get in trouble?" I glance around, uneasy.

He chuckles, his dimples on full display. "Why not? It's a slow Thursday, and you don't have to worry. They can't deduct your pay."

Touché.

Colton grabs the keys to the Southern Salvage truck and tells Franny we're headed to Gose Pike for a roller coaster. She snaps her head up, eyes wide, which does not ease my nerves.

"Seatbelt." He gestures.

And just like that, we're headed to Gose Pike. Other than the command to buckle up, he says nothing else the entire way. We take a left off the main road and enter the bypass. A bit closer to the outskirts of Broadwater, about fifteen minutes in, he puts on the blinker and turns onto Gose Pike. A wicked grin splits his face as he accelerates.

Colton Sturgest was not kidding when he called this road a roller coaster. He accelerates over the first hill—and there are plenty—and my stomach sinks, then catapults into a blissful feeling of weightlessness. I gasp at the sensation and laugh despite myself. Colton has a wide grin full of perfectly aligned, beautiful white teeth, which I'd admire more but we're at the next hill. My stomach flutters and flutters and flutters, and it isn't just from the hills. Gose Pike is long. I'm not mad about it.

Finally, Colton slows the car and loops back to the bypass, our field trip over. I rest my head against the headrest and grin.

He stares at me for a sec then swallows, his Adam's apple bobbing. "I thought you could use a good roller-coaster."

"Thanks," I say softly, glad he's unaware of my fluttering heartbeat.

He nods. In no time at all we're back at the shop. Franny offers a knowing grin when we walk in the door, a curious look in her eyes. Uncomfortable under her scrutiny, my cheeks warm. She shakes her head as I follow Colton to the Waymaker Station so he can show me how to insert the lights in the bottles and connect them on a circuit. When we've set up, it looks like a giant, wiry mess.

As we start to clean up, he stops and rubs a hand across the back of his neck. "Hey, have a seat for a sec." He pulls out the stools tucked under the Waymaker counter and motions for me to claim one.

Colton clears his throat. "Franny told me about your study session Wednesday. Look, I'm sorry about Kyra." He takes a deep breath and dives in. "Hadley, I… I owe you an apology." His forehead wrinkles and he struggles with what to say.

"For what?" I ask, genuinely confused and yeah, a little nervous. I glance down and force myself to stop picking at my pinky nail.

"For giving you the cold shoulder for the past month. When we first met, I was still reeling from being cheated on, and you gave me the impression you had cheated—"

"*What*?! When? I don't remember that?" I squeak out. My eyebrows flirt with my hairline.

"Sorry, I—" He takes a moment to collect himself, then starts again. "We were talking about the printing press, and I tried to warn you to be careful since it's pretty hard to cheat death. You responded 'Meh, I've cheated before. Ain't no thang.'"

He mimics my posture perfectly, one hand on his hip and the other flailing carelessly in the air. He even raises his voice an octave. His impression of me is spot on. And mortifying.

"I assumed you were implying you'd cheated on your boyfriend. I didn't give you a fair chance after that. I thought you were cold-hearted because you'd cheated, like Kyra." He takes a huge breath of air and crosses his fingers together on top of his head, surrendering cobra-style.

"Duuudddde. I meant I ate dessert before dinner or jaywalked or something." Holy heck, where has all the oxygen gone?

Colton shrugs and the magnitude of his accusation sinks in.

"Oh-my-gosh-I-would-never-cheat-ever-in-my-life-I-can't-even-imagine-doing-something-like-that!" This spills out so quickly it runs together as one massive word. "Seriously. I've never even really dated. Most people make fun of me because the whole idea of dating horrifies me."

"I noticed." He deadpans.

"So… how long did you two date?" My voice grows timid with fear that I'm treading on eggshells.

He swallows. "Two years. She cheated for almost a month before I found out."

"*Two years?*" I blink so my eyes don't bulge out of their sockets. "I can't even go on two dates." I blush at my self-deprecation and the situation in general.

"There you go, always making everything about you." He smirks as he teases. There's that dimple again.

"I'm sorry that happened to you." And after a pause, I blurt out, "But boys are kind of terrifying actually. And the hotter the guy, the scarier." I jerk my hand to cover my flaming hot face, embarrassed. I'm an idiot.

He barks out a laugh, then gently pulls my hands down. "I've been a jerk to you for weeks and you don't seem the least bit afraid of me."

My jaw drops. "Colton Sturgest, you're scarier than a pop quiz on Friday the thirteenth on the same day your college admissions essay is due," I blurt. Surely my face is a splotchy red tomato. I'd give the ground one hundred bucks to swallow me up right now. But the cocky, million-dollar grin on his face? I don't regret that. Not even a little.

"Yeah?" His smirk highlights his dimple.

"Yeah. When all that falls on a full moon." I don't know when I grew so bold, but now my face is on fire. My heart might beat out of my chest. Colton rolls his eyes at my mortification, then turns to pick up another bottle and we resume our tasks. For half a silent hour, we connect lights and twist wire ends together. I connect the wires to a switch, flip it to "on" and then...

"Let there be light." I whoop when they twinkle from their bottles. My enthusiasm earns me a fist bump from Colton. He pulls out his phone, takes a picture of me surrounded by bottles and fairy lights, and posts with wild abandonment, his thumbs frantically hash tagging.

I shine the lit bottle in my hands into Colton's steel-blue eyes. "Well, I'm definitely not a cheater, and I'm glad you've finally seen the light." I offer a cheesy grin, proud of my pun.

He holds out a hand. "Friends?"

I shake his callused, giant boy hand. "Friends." It's a lovely truce, really. I startle and let go of his handshake when Franny coughs behind us.

"Do you want some help getting ready for your date tomorrow? I could stop by your house, or you could come here. Either works." Franny's face is bright with excitement.

I do *not* want the poor guy picking me up harassed by Libby and Patrick. Or worse, Greg.

"How about here? Would that be ok?"

"Sounds like a plan." And because it's five p.m., I clean up, pack up, and tell the Sturgests' goodnight, waving goodbye to Twinkles on my way out. This time, her overalls are shining like a pink neon sun.

Friday, in the staff room, Franny paints some fancy lip gloss that smells like heaven and cotton candy all over my lips. I generally feel like a clown in a ton of makeup, so I beg Franny to go easy. She reaches for the mascara–again– when Colton and his aunt Lesley walk into the room. Colton's mouth turns down, his expression pinched. Is my outfit too much? I bet I look ridiculous.

Lesley, however, is beaming. "Hadley, some guy named Peter is here to pick you up. Lemme say, he is G-

O-R-G-E-O-U-S. Don't do anything Mike and I wouldn't do." She winks and Franny rolls her eyes.

I check my lacquered lips in an antique mirror and adjust my denim skirt, run a brush through my hair one final time and look to Franny for approval. She gives me a thumbs up, then I take a deep breath and wonder exactly why dating is so scary.

"You're a dude, Colton. Do you think I look ok?" I hold my arms out and do a turn, hoping for his validation. Colton shrugs then turns away.

I deflate a little. Never mind then. Here goes nothing.

Nothing was an excellent way to describe the date. Or half-date. The next morning, I'm sitting on the oldest, coolest (and only) butcher block I've ever seen in all my seventeen years, double checking bottles and counting lights when Franny calls from the front.

"One sec," I yell, afraid that if I stop I'll lose count and have to start all over. I clean up my space and head to the front, but my guard goes up when I see their expressions.

"What?" I'm going to feign ignorance with a shred of hope that we don't have to discuss my disastrous evening with Peter.

Franny starts the inquisition. "Sooooo… tell us about your date. Based on what I heard from his sister, I definitely need some clarifying details."

"Did you get your first ever kiss?" Turns out Colton does an epic valley girl impersonation, too. "Was it, like, super-duper romantic?" His eyes blink rapidly and he places both hands over his chest. What a dork.

"Ugh. High school gossip. You'd think a new school would change things." Again, different dog, same stinky poo. "Why? What did you hear?"

"Um, well, let's see. I heard he called you the 'human cactus,'" Franny says this last part slowly, as if narrating a Cliff's Note version of "Awkward Dating for Idiots."

"What does that even mean?"

Franny rolls her eyes and enunciates each word slowly and deliberately, as if I'm dense. "It means he thinks you're pretty and interesting but, like a cactus, everyone knows you DO NOT TOUCH!"

Colton's amusement seems to fade at her words, and I notice his jaw clench.

"Yeah, there's not going to be a second date considering I didn't even finish the first. While we looked over the dessert menu, he was crass enough to ask how far I'd ever been with a guy."

"What?" Colton snaps, his features tight. "Please tell me you're joking." He's really staring at me now, concern evident in his eyes.

"I told him I once flew as far as Hawaii to tour Pearl Harbor with the Captain, then I ordered the most expensive dessert on the menu, excused myself to the restroom, and walked out the front door."

Franny's jaw drops while Colton shakes his head, both pleased with my response. "Taylor pegged him as just your type…" Franny says as she shakes her head.

"I don't have a 'type.' And, unfortunately, Taylor doesn't have the gift of discernment," I explain. "Plus, I've never even been kissed." My mouth works faster than my brain sometimes.

"I know, I'm pathetic. I mean, I've been, like, chicken pecked, you know like sixth graders at a well chaperoned dance, but never like, *kissed*, you know, *properly*." I back up against the counter and my arms fall to my sides, listless. My rambling mouth needs a set of brakes.

"Properly," Colton repeats, his voice a mixture of amazement and astonishment. Is he mocking me, or in a deep state of shock, or both?

I shake my head. I can't even talk anymore because I know if I open my mouth to try to say anything, it won't work. More awkward will spew out. I suffer from word vomit sometimes.

"Never? You're joking." He's still staring at me like I've grown a second head.

"Wait—you've never even had a New Year's kiss?" Franny asks. "A special Valentine's Day smooch?"

I stare back at them, trying to keep my cool, but I can tell my cheeks are growing warm. "Nah... but last week I had one of those white chocolate Hershey kisses with peppermint—you know, the Christmas ones? It was *spectacular.*"

Thanks be-eth unto the good Lord, a customer clears his throat to get Colton's attention. I waste no time finding a job—any job—to get away from this mortifying conversation.

###

When I report to work Tuesday afternoon, there is a pack of Hershey's peppermint kisses at my workstation. I will not swoon x 500. But I do, a lot.

I head to the front to find Colton and nearly smack into Kyra, holding the hand of an adorable little boy in a wheelchair, a giant from Halloween Town in his lap. Colton walks over, runs a hand through his hair, and greets his guests. Now invisible, I quietly excuse myself and head back to the Waymaker Station. I work on approximately zero bottles while I try to figure out what's going on.

CHAPTER 12

Pot Stickers & Heart Palpitations

»» ———————————— ««

By Thursday afternoon, that Halloween Town bag poking out from behind the staff room door has grown an attitude and taunts me. When I ask Franny about it her cryptic response is "That's a loaded question and one I would *not* ask Colton," followed by an impressive eye roll. Noted. And not at all helpful.

Halloween has never been a big holiday for me, a mere excuse to eat a ton of junk and dress up for funsies, but mostly a blip of a gateway day to gear up for Thanksgiving and Christmas. Later, however, when Libby and Patrick overhear me asking Karie about Halloween Town, their interest is piqued. They don't want to go to Halloween Town. They want to start making their costumes. Karie is a Pinterest Parent. I suspect this will not be the end of their enthusiasm, so I head to the kitchen as it's my night to cook.

Saturday is rainy and gross, but not so dreary I can't put a cute mini raincoat on Twinkles. Karie cleaned out Libby's old doll clothes and said I could have it. Twinkles looks even more adorable, and I didn't even think that was possible.

Other than the gnome mini-fashion show, it's a slow morning on account of the weather. Colton has created an inventory game with the Southern Salvage T-shirts, usually a constant battle to keep in stock since they sell like hotcakes to tourists. We're yelling out item numbers and tossing the shirts to and from one another when I attempt a blind pass quarterback style. Who should I accidentally hit? Mr. Sturgest. As in, the stoic, scary Mr. Sturgest.

He blinks.

I shrink.

He picks the shirt up off the floor, places it with a "thunk" on the counter and walks off without a word. Colton exhales loudly, then laughs so hard he has trouble catching his breath. It's a lovely sound, but I wish my misery weren't his entertainment. His laugh gets the attention of Mike, who saunters over to the counter wearing a green shirt with a pickle that reads "Dill With It." He's just in time to witness Colton throw another shirt my way, only for it to thwack me in the side of my head. *Of course* I trip and land in an awkward heap on the floor.

"The Holy Spirit slap some sense into ya?" Mike looks down as he looms over me, and I let out a groan. I peek at Colton, who's bent over with his hands on his knees, crying from laughing so hard. Mike shrugs and wanders off, unfazed.

Colton wipes his cheeks with the edges of his hoodie as he makes his way over to me, shaking his head. "You don't need me to embarrass you, do you? You're perfectly capable of that yourself." He offers a gorgeous grin and a calloused hand, then pulls me up effortlessly. That zing of electricity is still there, and I wonder if he feels it too. If he does, he doesn't show it.

Embarrassed, but thrilled to see this side of Colton, I wipe the dust from my palms on my jeans and change the subject. "Shouldn't I be working on the lights?"

"You absolutely should be, but Mike used all the silicon carbide discs yesterday and the next shipment isn't due until tomorrow. You shouldn't try to smooth out any of the bottles' edges with regular sandpaper or you could cut yourself."

I go still. Instantly, my palms start to sweat.

"Uh… you could work on the light circuits." He looks at me funny, brow all furrowed, and then I see the lightbulb click on. "Let me guess… You're afraid of blood?"

I try not to shudder but fail. "Makes me a bit queasy, is all." It makes me a whole lot of queasy, but I've given him enough tease-worthy arsenal this morning.

"We all try to be careful–Grandpa and Uncle Mike preach safety first, but accidents happen, right?" He rolls up his sleeves to reveal a faded, puffy scar on his forearm.

I cringe away at first, then hesitate as I reach out and touch the scarred tissue, softly rubbing my finger down the length of the shiny, silver-pink skin. Colton inhales and goosebumps rise on the surface of his skin. I pull my hand back, self-conscious.

"*Oh!* I–I'm sorry. I–" Gulp. " That looks like it must've hurt."

"Not too bad." His voice is gravelly, his eyes trained on me.

"How did that happen?" I bite my lip, afraid of what he might say.

He winces. "Had a little run in with the rotary sander. It was a stupid mistake. Really stupid, honestly." The corners of his mouth turn down for a moment, but his smile quickly returns, probably because I'm biting my lip in concern. "I'm fine now, Hads."

His dimple appears, and I am the living embodiment of the expression "weak in the knees." I have a new appreciation for the counter I've leaned up against.

He clears his throat. "Well, you work on the lights, and I'll finish up with the shirts."

"Sounds like a plan."

Sounds like a plan? I wish the Holy Spirit had slapped some sense into me. Or some flirting skills.

I work for a solid hour, tangled in a knotted mess of wires and lights, with a twisted mess of a stomach to match. How does someone with a severe lack of dating skills and a fear of all things boy, fight off feelings for her attractive, funny, and surprisingly sweet mentor? In secret, for starters.

"So." Colton is back...

"So..." And my shift is coming to an end.

He takes a tiny step toward me. "What are you doing the rest of the day?" There's curiosity in his eyes, and something else. Vulnerability?

"Karie offered me her bike so I could visit Nonny, but I don't think that's going to happen anymore." I glance out the rain splattered front windows.

"I can take you."

I blink at his unexpected offer. "You don't have to do that." I politely refuse, but then again, I'm desperate to see Nonny.

"You sure? We could pick up some lunch and take it to her."

Nonny, food, and a side of Colton? "Actually, yeah, that sounds kind of awesome."

"Great. Let me finish cleaning up the front counter and I'll grab my keys. Meet me out back in five?"

I give my best nonchalant "Sure" and make my way to the staff room to grab my bag. I also check to see if there is an AED in case I succumb to cardiac arrest since my heart is beating entirely too fast to be considered healthy. Breathe.

"You ready?" Either Colton is crazy efficient or that was the fastest five minutes of my life.

"Ready." I head toward the Southern Salvage van.

"No van today–not a work errand." He holds open the passenger door to a silver Jeep and motions for me to get in. I do, and I'm hit by a wave of eau de Colton, all minty and soapy clean, with a hint of Waymaker Station sawdust and wood finish. It's a real effort not to take a deep breath.

"What's Nonny's favorite food?" He fiddles with the auxiliary cord while he hooks his phone up and opens Spotify.

"She's not picky, but her tastes changed after all her chemo treatments. Chinese?"

"Chinese it is." He drives through Panda Express, ordering three huge entrees, pot-stickers, egg rolls, and three sweet teas. I reach in my bag to pull out my debit card, but he shoots me a look and waves off my offering. Nonny is going to love him. I'm just trying not to like him so much.

###

The distinct "old person smell" overwhelms my senses. I can hear Nonny before I see her, she's got the TV so loud. When I see Nonny in her new nursing home room, I freeze. She's so thin and frail, even her hair hangs limp, not at all like she prefers. I squeeze my eyes shut and open them again, willing myself to be strong while Nonny can't.

She's wearing her "Go Army, Beat Navy" sweater and a knitted USNA beanie, complete with pom. And she can pull it off 'cause she's my Nonny, and Nonny is awesome.

"Is here okay?" Colton sets the bags of food, food I doubt Nonny will be interested in, on the small table beside her window. He pulls a seat out for me and I sit automatically. Nonny stirs and smiles. Why I expected her to be incoherent, I'm not sure, but she greets me by name and even says hi to Colton.

"What a pleasant surprise. I wasn't expecting anyone to come out in this yucky mess."

"A little rain isn't going to stop Hadley here from seeing her Nonny." Colton winks at me, his gift for making a heavy moment a touch lighter is truly special. "Can I fix your pillow for you? Help you sit up?"

Colton helps her adjust her pillow, then cuts one of the potstickers in miniscule pieces and unwraps the cellophane of her fork. "My grandmother stayed in this very same nursing home. I used to come visit and play cards with her all the time."

I swallow the lump in my throat and blink back tears. He *used* to visit. So, his grandmother must have passed away. I fidget with the cuffs on my pullover to distract myself.

"Hadley, dear, I had a dream that you got that Naval internship you obsessed over all summer. Craziest thing ever–the Captain visited from heaven to celebrate at Puckett's with you and Taylor. My mind has a weird imagination. It was nice to see the Captain, though." She finishes two tiny bites and Colton helps her sip through a straw on her overbed table. He looks at me, curious.

"That's a fun dream, Nonny. I haven't even had time to think of the Naval Internship. Doesn't matter much anyway, huh?" Funny how that was only about two months ago and how much has changed since then. I choke back tears in my throat and will myself to keep it together. While I can, I need to enjoy my Nonny. If she can have a good attitude, so can I. She might have a happy spirit, but her body is tired, and she goes quiet again.

"What have you been praying for, sweetheart?" She always asks me this, but it feels like too personal of a question to answer in front of Colton.

"School, my internship project, Taylor. Umm... Libby running cross-country. You. I pray for you every day." I give her hand a gentle squeeze.

"Thank you, Hadley. Pray for peace and comfort. My healing won't come this side of heaven, but it will come. And I want you to be happy for me when it does."

"Yes ma'am." Can't argue with that. And I don't think either of us has the energy to debate anything right now anyway.

"No matter what, sugar, God is still good." Her voice and her eyes hold so much conviction as she says this, and then she rests her head against the pillow again.

"God is still good." My response sounds so weak and comes out in barely a whisper.

Colton cups a hand around my elbow and whispers, "I can start cleaning this up if you want to say anything else before we leave."

I nod and cross my arms, then rest them against her bed rail as her eyes smile at me.

"I love you, Nonny."

"I love you too, Hadley."

Spent from our visit, she closes her eyes. When her breathing grows deep and even, I kiss her on her forehead and follow Colton back to his Jeep.

###

I'm Facetiming Taylor to tell her all about my afternoon visit with Nonny and Colton when a knock sounds on the door. Karie pokes her head in to say hello to Taylor and hands me a piece of certified mail. Holy cow, my breath catches when I see the return address: *The Office of Naval Research.* When Karie leaves, Taylor has to clear her throat to get my attention.

"Hello? You spaced out on me for a sec." I hold up the letter and she squeals. Then I squeal. There is a lot of squealing going on here. "Open it, open it, open it!"

With shaky hands I tear open the envelope and pull out the letter. A deep breath and I read…

October 1, 2024

Re: Hadley Edwards

Dear Miss Hadley Edwards:

The Office of Naval Research is pleased to offer you an educational internship opportunity. You will intern under the guidance of Dr. Hobson. This eight-week position is located in Arlington, Virginia at the Office of Naval Research. As you will receive academic credit for this position, there will be no remuneration. Additionally, students do not receive benefits as part of their internship program.

For this position, your major duties will include assisting laboratory personnel in their scientific and technological research as it relates to the Department of the Navy. Your schedule will be approximately 12 hours per week beginning Monday, June 2, 2025. Your assignment will conclude on Friday, July 25, 2025.

Please review, sign, and return via mail to confirm acceptance, no later than the

close of business on Monday, November 1, 2024.

Shanna M. Heath.

Congratulations and welcome to the Department of Naval Research!

Sincerely,

CR Christopher Royce

CR Johnathan Sawyer

cc: Major-General Richard Hobson, Ph.D.

I accept the above offer, and will begin on: Monday, June 2, 2025.

_____/_____

Signature   Date

"Oh my gosh, Hadley! You did it! Do you know what this means? You're coming back home to Maryland–you can spend your summer interning here with me! You know my mom will let you stay with us. Are you stoked or what?"

Kinda. Yeah. Shouldn't I be? I should... so why am I not as excited as I imagined I would be? I'm not even half as excited as Taylor.

That's when I hear it. Libby's feet running down the hall, followed by the slam of her bedroom door. She must have overheard the entire conversation. I take a deep breath and close my eyes. This isn't how I imagined this moment would feel at all. Why am I experiencing guilt about achieving something I thought I wanted and worked so hard to get?

After a few days of processing the offer, I still have zero clarity. None. Tuesday afternoon at Southern Salvage, Colton is out on a pick-up and I fill Franny in on my news. She congratulates me and I feign excitement; I don't know how to explain my complex emotions—I barely understand them myself.

CHAPTER 13

Decisions, Decisions…

»» ———————————— ««

"My advice for young people is, study what you love and intern in what you want to do. And I think it's okay to pivot as many times as you need to."

-Eva Chen, Director of Fashion, Instagram

Mr. Howardson has a stain on the top of his striped, red tie and I can't decide if it would be more polite to ignore it or mention it so he can spot clean it. It's the last week of the month and time for my mid-week check-in with my advisor. I trace my finger across the carvings on the top of my student desk.

"So, Miss Edwards, tell me about the progress on your…" he flips open my folder and double checks the reports I've submitted, "your light fixture." He smiles, his bushy salt and pepper brows lifting with his grin.

"Well, I have all the bottles I need, thanks to a sponsorship from Bluegrass Bottling. Colton taught me to cut them properly, but they're not all ready. And I've learned how to insert the lights. I still have no idea how to connect the bottle lights together and hang them."

"Yes, I saw some of the posts on Southern Salvage's Instagram Page. Your progress is generating quite a bit of likes, I've noticed."

Mr. Howardson has social media.

And I don't.

"Yes sir."

"Tell me how you're getting along with your mentor."

At his words, my face flames and I pray he can't see my blush.

I blink, unsure of what exactly he wants to know.

"Your mentor, Colton, expressed a few minor concerns in your mid-project evaluation."

He *what?*

"Overall, the report was fair and objective. Based on your grades and student information, the few issues he did bring to attention seem out of character for you, Miss Edwards." He licks his finger to turn his report to the next page. "It says you 'require constant supervision due to lack of project-related knowledge' and 'lack leadership skills and the ability to effectively communicate in regard to the completion of the project.'" He studies me over the rim of his bifocals. It's unnerving.

"Mr. Howardson, I'm not sure what to say." Don't panic. Don't panic. Don't panic. I choose my next words with care. "I wish my mentor had expressed his concerns to me before he wrote his report. I would've worked on my shortcomings."

He clears his throat. "Hadley, is Colton aware of your grandmother's condition and your unique situation at home?"

That's a nice way to describe being up-ended.

"Yes sir." I don't want pity. I want to scream at Colton for his harsh words. And figure out why he wrote them in the first place!

"Perhaps he wasn't aware when he wrote his report– everyone is due a little grace, including, and especially, you." Odd how receiving sympathy sometimes feels like shame.

He places the report back in my folder and sets it on his desk, then rests his glasses on top and clasps his hands together. "Well, I'm pleased with your progress, and I don't see any glaring red flags. I'd like to remind you that the Fall Festival will be here before you know it. Blink and a month will pass."

"Yes sir."

"Anything else you'd like to share?"

Sweet mercy, a chance to humbly brag and save a little face after that dismal report. "I was offered an internship at the Naval Lab in Annapolis. My grandfather was a professor at the Naval Academy."

Mr. Howardson doesn't speak for a moment. I break eye contact and stir in my seat, uncomfortable with his silence.

"Very impressive, Miss Edwards. I didn't realize that's something you're interested in." Is that a question in his voice? "And are you planning to accept?"

"Oh, I could never consider turning it down. It's important for me to honor the Captain's legacy." I stare down at my hands in my lap.

"Which I respect, but is this internship something you're interested in or is it something you think your grandfather would have wanted? I hope I'm not overstepping my bounds, but as a grandfather myself, I'd like to think he'd want you to choose what's best for *you*."

Interesting. I chew the side of my lip. His words send me back to a time in my childhood when the Captain took me to the Storm Brother's Ice Cream Factory near the Navy Yard. Always eager to please him, I ordered Butter-Pecan, just like him.

Towering over me, his eyes sharp but warm, his gravelly voice gently encouraged me. "You can order anything you'd like, sweetheart. This old codger isn't into rainbow sprinkles, but that doesn't mean you can't have them. Choose the flavor that brings you the most joy."

I remember mustering all my courage to order a colorful double scoop of bubble gum and cotton candy. His tough exterior gave way to a tender moment as he patted my head affectionately, a proud gleam in his eye.

I blink away the memory. *Is* the Naval Lab internship something I'm truly interested in?

Before I can respond to Mr. Howardson's loaded statement, the bell rings and I'm politely excused.

###

After school, Libby begs for a pre-church run. We have to make it short so we can shower and change before dinner. I don't realize I'm running so hard until she pants and begs me to slow down. These internship thoughts are eating away at my brain. On the bright side, they're a great distraction from focusing on Colton's less-than-favorable report or Nonny's declining health. What would Nonny tell me to do about Colton? What would she say about the internship offer?

"Sorry, Libby." I slow my pace. "What game topic would you like to pick today?"

"Halloween costumes!" Definitely should have seen that coming.

I start. "Angel."

"Ballerina."

"Clown."

"Hadley, are you going to move back to Maryland?"

That?

I did *not* see that coming. Kinda thought she might say "dinosaur."

I slow to a walk and catch my breath. "Huh? What made you ask that?"

"Because I heard Taylor say you could live with her. You don't like being my sister?" Her bottom lip quivers. Dang.

I drop down to one knee on the sidewalk and look her in the eyes. "That's something Taylor said. It wasn't something I even thought of." But now that I have, I have no idea what to do. "And that internship isn't permanent, it's only for six weeks. I wouldn't be leaving forever, even if I did accept the position."

Her shoulders fall from her ears. "Okay," she mumbles.

"And Libby, I love being your sister."

She grabs my neck and I fall back into an awkward sitting position on my tush. Pacified, Libby helps me up, grabs my hand, and we turn around to walk back, the run forgotten.

"Let's go eat a gigantic snack." Libby's statement comes out more like a command.

Psh. Who wouldn't like being her sister?

###

After youth group, where I avoided Franny like the plague because I absolutely was not ready to discuss the infamous report, I Facetime Taylor and share all the information Mr. Howardson unloaded on me.

"Whoa, harsh words from the male model." Taylor always shoots me straight.

"Ya think? I have to go there tomorrow. What am I supposed to do?"

"When did he write the report? Do you think he even remembers it?"

"No clue."

"It's just… call me crazy, but I'm pretty sure he likes you. Like, *likes* you." Her expression is tense, like she's trying to solve a riddle.

"Yep. You're crazy. Coocoo-for-Cocoa-Puffs, whack-a-doodle-nutzo."

"I'm serious. I'm not trying to set you up on some random date. This is Colton."

At that, I lounge back against the teal pillows stacked on my bed and twirl a strand of loose hair around my fingers, contemplating her words.

Taylor continues. "Some of those social media posts where you're both in the shot are pretty swoon worthy. And didn't he take you on some roller-coaster and visit Nonny with you? I know I'm not crazy. I'm right."

"Hadwey. Can I have some Cocoa Puffs? Pwease." Patrick is standing, bare bummed, in the doorway to my room.

"Uhhh, I better go get Patrick some cereal…"

"And some under-roos." Taylor is grinning at the current situation, which lightens my spirits a little.

"Why don't we go ask your mom? Later, Taylor." I sign off and lead Patrick to the kitchen, with a quick detour to the laundry room on the way.

###

Thursday is such a weird day. I finally make it to Southern Salvage—been dreading it since my meeting with Howardson and the revelation of that punk evaluation. Mike greets me at the door, takes one look at my expression, and starts shouting "AFA, AFA!" before he disappears to the back.

Franny steps out of the staff room, concerned. "Where is she?" she whispers.

I look around the otherwise empty WayMaker Station. "Who?"

"Mike gave his infamous 'Angry Female Alert.' I only see you."

Oh. I'm the AFA. I deflate.

"Mike's a pseudo-misogynistic clown. Are you upset about something?" Her eyes go wide. "Is Nonny okay?"

That question certainly helps put things into perspective. "Nonny's fine. Colton gave me a negative evaluation. Mr. Howardson read it over with me yesterday."

"Colton did what?" Franny takes a step back and her eyes widen.

"I did what?" Ah yes, it's Benedict Arnold himself.

"Would you look at the time?" Franny's shrill voice reveals her cowardice.

"Where's the AFA?" Colton doesn't realize he's poked the bear. He points to me, eyes wide. "You? You're the AFA? No way." And he has the gall to laugh. *Laugh.* Fortunately, he's blessed with at least enough wisdom to know when to stop. "What's wrong?" And bless his precious heart, those pursed lips of his almost make me believe his concern is genuine.

Almost.

I square my shoulders back and lift my chin. "Allow me to *effectively communicate* that I don't require your constant *supervision.* I'm perfectly capable of completing my project without a grumpy, spiteful babysitter." Cue the stupid mad-tears that decide to cloud my angry vision.

Recognition dawns in his frustratingly beautiful eyes. He winces and turns his head, seemingly embarrassed. At least he has the decency to show some remorse. "The report."

"The report. The one that counts for a portion of my grade. That's the one."

"I'm sorry."

"Yes, you are." With that sass, I turn to march off to my workspace. I hope my back to his face effectively communicates that our conversation is over.

"Hadley, wait." The desperation in his voice stops me. "I wrote that over two weeks ago. Before I 'saw the light' as you put it." He runs his fingers through his messy hair and exhales. "My anger at someone else, and who I *thought* you were, it got the best of me."

"So, you don't usually write hateful, unfair reports? Those are just for me?" I cross my arms and bite the inside of my lip, so *my* anger doesn't get the best of *me*.

"My report was unprofessional, and—"

"And cruel."

"I messed up." He sighs in defeat and his eyes plead for forgiveness. "And I'm sorry."

I stare at him, letting the silence linger a tad too long, and wait until he starts to squirm under my scrutiny. He repeats himself. "I'm sorry, Hadley."

"I'm not the type of person who would cheat. I'm truly sorry that happened to you—no one deserves to be treated like that—but I don't deserve to have you take your hurt out on me. I'm not a punching bag."

"No, you're not. And you're right, you don't deserve that. You're so much better than what I wrote in that stupid report." His Adam's apple bobs as he swallows. "I'll submit a new report to Mr. Howardson tonight."

That would certainly help. There's another long pause, and the silence drags on until I can't stand it. "Well, you've sufficiently groveled. I suppose I could forgive you."

That earns me a slow, glorious grin. "Yeah?

"Yeah."

"Thanks, Hadley." It's his turn to stare at me, apparently, and now I squirm under his scrutiny. He takes a step and playfully grazes my shoulder, nudging me back towards the Waymaker Station. "Ready to get to work?" I was ready, until he hit me in the feels with the shoulder bump.

"Always," I lie.

"Hadley?"

"Colton?"

"What are you wearing?"

I follow his gaze down to my feet and blush. "It was trench warfare reenactment day in A.P. US History. Mr. Howardson passed out these hideous dyed socks with the words 'Trench Foot' embroidered on the cuff to symbolize the plight of WWI soldiers." I hold my foot up and wiggle my toes.

Colton nods and then starts to chuckle. "I thought you wore wool socks because you had cold feet about your project." He crosses his arms across his chest and lifts his square chin.

"*Har har.* Maybe I wore fun socks because I'm a sock star." I shrug haughty and stare down my nose at his feet. "And by the way, your sock has a hole in it."

"What? How would you even know?" He gestures to his steel toe.

"How else would you get your foot in it?" One hand anchored to my hip, I use the other to pat myself on the back.

He blows out puffed up cheeks and releases an exaggerated breath. "Wow. That was terrible."

"That's fair," I concede, but I can't help grinning at our banter. With the report issue out of the way, it's as if a huge weight has lifted off my shoulders. "You ready to work?"

"Yep. Sock it to me." Ha! I didn't expect Colton to be so punny. This version is much more likable than the one I spent most of my day fuming over.

He lifts a box of lights up from off the floor and sets them on the counter with a dull thud. "But before we get lost in the vast abyss of sock puns, I'll change the subject. What are you doing this weekend?"

I pick up the lights and start organizing them while we talk. "I'm supposed to go to an ACT workshop Saturday afternoon. College admissions, the ACTs, *especially* the Naval Internship… they were such a big deal to me before Nonny got sick."

He nods. "And now?"

"Now I don't know. I want to do well on this project. I want to be a good sister, which feels weird to say out loud." I laugh despite myself. "Libby freaked out the other night when she heard Taylor mention me moving back to Maryland."

Colton's hand goes still on the bottle he's sanding. "I thought you weren't pursuing that internship anymore. Isn't that what Nonny said?"

"I… I don't know. That same afternoon I received an offer." We both grow quiet, and I wish I could read Colton's mind. "Penny for your thoughts?" My words come out almost as quiet.

"Libby isn't the only one who doesn't want you to go back to Maryland." He rubs his thumb against his temple. "Sorry. That was selfish. I'm on a roll today."

I can't believe what I'm hearing. "You... don't?"

He shakes his head. "I don't." I bite my lip. This moment, it's like a spell, and I don't want to ruin it. He lifts a hand and gently tucks an errant strand of hair behind my ear, then looks at my lips. My heart bangs like it might beat out of my chest. As he begins to slowly lean in–

"AFA! I repeat, AFA!" Mike whisper-yells as he passes by. I startle and straighten, the moment gone so fast it's almost as if it never happened.

"Another AFA?" Colton and I look toward the front.

And there stands a frazzled looking Karie holding Patrick on her hip with Libby beside her.

CHAPTER 14

One Scary Misunderstanding

»» ———————————— ««

Karie puffs a stray strand of auburn hair out of her distressed eyes and sets a squirmy Patrick on the floor. The reflection from his light-up sneakers glows bright against the concrete floor, all the way to where I'm standing. Puppy dog eyes look up at me while he pulls on the edges of my cuffs.

"Pwease, Hadley, pwease say you'll dwess up and twick-o-tweat with us!" He jumps with excitement, and I smile at his enthusiasm.

"Um, sure. Yeah, sounds like fun." How can anyone say no to an adorable four-year-old?

Karie's shoulders sag with immediate relief. What have I agreed to? "Are you sure, Hadley? You don't have to do this if you don't want to." Her eyes say otherwise.

"No, I want to. Really." I think.

I hear Colton whisper "sucker" under his breath before he walks away, shaking his head as he goes. He might be right, but I'll cherish that toothy grin Patrick gave me when I conceded to… whatever I'd conceded to.

Later that evening, Karie invites me to her sewing nook in a crafty corner of the basement. For a woman so meticulously organized, this place is a mess. There are rolls of vinyl strewn around a Cricut, a spool of ribbons dangling crooked from a hook on the wall, and several glue guns mixed in with a set of markers Crayola would envy. On a corner cabinet sits a random framed picture and judging by the elderly Asian couple in the picture, I don't think she's ever changed out the photo from the canned store version. She opens a cabinet and pulls out a dusty sewing machine, super similar to the one Nonny has.

"I can barely sew a straight line, but the kids and I love our homemade costume tradition. I don't know what I would have done if you'd said no." Grateful rays of sunshine emit from her eyes.

"Nonny taught me how to sew. I can help."

Karie's eyes bulge out of their sockets. "PTL. I have literally won the stepdaughter lottery." Seems a little much, but I'll take it.

"So, what am I supposed to dress up as?" In my mind I picture a cute character from one of the Pete the Cat books Patrick loves, or an Avenger since he has all the action figures and enjoys battling it out every night before bed.

Karie gives me a sheepish look. "So, one of your dad's favorite movies is Men in Black. They watch it all the time together. Patrick and Libby want to be agents, and–"

"I can pull that off, easy-peasy."

"—and they want you to be the giant roach spider alien thingy they kill at the end."

What the…

I blink.

Karie shows me the four brown turtlenecks she picked up at the store. Seriously?

I help her cut off the sleeves from three of them, then sew them to the remaining one. The motion of gently guiding the fabric over the presser foot and the soft, repetitive clicking sound coming from the machine takes me right back to my living room in Annapolis. For a brief moment my vision blurs as the sudden waves of nostalgia and loss wash over me. I swallow the lump in my throat and hope Karie doesn't notice.

We use thread to hand sew the sleeves to one another so that when I move my arms the others will move with them. Finally, we craft a hideous headband with brown pipe-cleaners for the antenna and complete the look with yucky, poo-brown sweatpants to complete the ensemble. Ew.

"Thank you, Hadley, for agreeing to dress up with Patrick and Libby. Saturday night, I'll help you with your make-up and the extra eyeballs." My own eyeballs bulge out of their sockets. The *what?*

"Happy to help. I should go work on some school stuff and give Taylor and Nonny a call." Tomorrow is club day so I don't have much homework. And I already called Nonny and Taylor, but I can't handle any more brown cockroach spider alien thingy. I call it a night and head to my room.

This Club Friday should be dubbed Freezing Friday. I'm not that upset about the change in weather because I have cute sweaters and won't need to shave my legs so much. The last week of October brings chills along with the excitement of planning for trick-or-treating with Patrick and Libby. I'm going to wear that big-sister badge of honor with pride. And stick-on eyeballs.

In art club, I'm sure Raven suspects my little crush on Colton. "What are you smiling at?"

When I point to myself, she rolls her eyes and laughs. "Yeah, you. You were staring off into space, smiling at nothing." Her eyes narrow and she smiles. "Spill."

My face grows hot, like the Jack-O-Lantern I'm painting for today's project. "Nah, it's nothing."

"Based on that blush you're rocking, I'd say it's something. *Ohmygosh*, you fell for your mentor, didn't you?"

"Raven!" I hiss. "Will you hush?" I look around frantically to see who might have overheard.

"I knew it the moment I saw those steamy Instagram posts. Is he a good kisser?"

"What? I don't know," I whisper.

"Oh." She deflates and her shoulders fall in disappointment. "So, is this more 'situationship' than 'relationship?' Have you had a DTR?"

"Huh?" She needs to speak English.

"Have you *defined the relationship*?"

What relationship? "No. But we had an almost kiss yesterday."

"Yep. Definitely a situationship. Those are fun, too, though." She nods thoughtfully and once again, I'm saved by the bell. I've never packed my bag so fast.

###

It's been a fun day, but I have to get to bed early because tomorrow morning I've got the ACT. I've done well on the test in the past, but tomorrow is my last chance to score a tiny bit higher. The big bad A-C-T used to freak me out, but moving six hundred miles to live with a new insta-fam while your Nonny fades away can put things into perspective.

I want to do well, though, because even two or three more points could mean hundreds of dollars in scholarship money. Something tells me Greg and Karie didn't budget for me to go to college. I need my brain to be quiet, so I use one of my stepmom's official guidance counselor suggestions and write all my worries down then throw the paper in the garbage.

It doesn't work. Like, at all.

Instead, I go to my trusty default method and pour my heart out to Jesus instead.

I wake in a fog after sleeping like a spanked baby. My Saturday morning routine usually includes interning at Southern Salvage—I'm bummed that I can't tell Colton and Franny about my Halloween plans. How sad that I never built up enough nerve to ask Colton about the Halloweentown bag he keeps tucked behind the staff room door, but I'm hoping I'll be lucky enough to find out today.

Normally I wouldn't stress about what to wear to the torture session that is standardized testing, but considering I'm planning to look hideous later, I take my time getting ready. Braid my hair, apply a touch of mascara and a thin layer of clear gloss, put on my favorite pair of jeans and a Patagonia fleece and I'm good to go. I grab my bag, my TI-84, and I even have time left to pick up an iced chai at

Mug Masters on the way. I ask Greg to go through the Kyra-free drive-through, though, 'cause I don't need bad mojo before the ACT.

"Does this outfit make my butt look big?" Taylor laughs as we Facetime and get ready. I'm sure my appearance is nothing less than disgusting, but based on the looks of admiration on Patrick and Libby's faces, it's worth it. I've got eight arms, googly eyes secured to my forehead with fake eyelash glue, icky brown sweatpants, and a chestnut pair of Karie's old Uggs. We even bought tinted hairspray in "chocolate" and teased my mane to crazy, messy heights. There is an electric energy in the air and—

We. Are. Ready.

They're adorable in their little suits, black ties, and sunglasses. They even have the knock-off "neuralizer" wand thingies in case they need to erase anyone's short-term memory.

I watch Taylor secure a bobby pin in her younger sister's ballerina bun before she says, "You guys have fun!" We sign off and grab our empty bags, ready for loads of confections and cavities-to-be.

Karie gives me directions on which streets to take and an epic helicopter-mom speech about only going to homes with lights on, never entering homes, blah blah blah. I thought she might actually pull out those kid leash things. But then, we're off. And I melt a little when they each take a hand as we head down the sidewalk (with flashlights and extra batteries, of course).

Two streets down and these bags are getting heavy. As their fearless older half-sister, I've been given bag duty and with all this extra weight, I'm pretty sure I can skip the gym tomorrow. Our third and final street is a doozy–super wealthy homes with insanely rich owners who give out full size candy bars. Or worse, toothbrushes in a vain attempt to counteract the candy. These homes are luxurious and spectacular, like the ones on the glossy covers of Nonny's magazines.

Patrick starts to fade, feet dragging, but his spirits remain high. The final mansion on the end of the street will be it for us, so we march up those steps and ring the ridiculously fancy, camera-embedded space doorbell.

And it's pretty much downhill from there.

Kyra answers in a stunning Cinderella ensemble, fancy updo, and sparkly, perfect make-up. I'd be willing to bet she has on actual glass slippers. She, too, could be on the glossy cover of a magazine. Her sickly-sweet smile beguiles a look of disdain, and when she takes in my outfit, she chokes back a laugh.

"Oh, wow. *Wow.* My prince charming has got to see this! Colton…" She bats her lengthy lashes and stares down at us past her prim, pointy nose.

My stomach drops when Colton, dressed in a tuxedo as a gorgeous Prince Charming, walks into the ginormous foyer. At first, he's distracted, pushing a young boy Patrick's age dressed as a coachman in a pumpkin decorated wheelchair. I recognize the boy from the day he and Kyra dropped off the Halloweentown Bag at Southern Salvage. The little guy takes in our group and a grin splits his adorable face. It's clear he loves it, two agents with their hideous alien spider cockroach.

I die a little inside when Colton makes eye contact– and I have a lot of eyes to choose from–and does a double take when he recognizes me. Guilt registers in those handsome blue orbs and his expression screams contrition. He swallows and his lips turn down, then he looks the other way, missing Kyra's smug smirk of satisfaction. Is it possible I *did* imagine our almost-kiss Thursday? I'm an idiot.

If Patrick and Libby's neuralizers worked, I'd use them on myself.

Patrick mercifully breaks the awkward silence with "Twick owr Tweat!" and Kyra glides gracefully to a massive crystal bowl. With perfectly manicured nails, she drops giant handfuls of expensive European chocolate brands

169

I've never heard of into their bags, her fully displayed ta-tas spilling out of the top of her beautiful, tailored dress as she bends to their height. It's enough to make me wonder if this chick has an actual fairy godmother.

This definitely seems more like a trick than a treat, and why does Colton have to look my way again as my eyes fill with tears? I thank my sweet Lord when Kyra closes the door in my face.

"Did you see all the candy she put in our bag? That was insane!" Agent Libby and Agent Patrick look at me with matching expressions, glee radiating from their huge, innocent eyes. I try my best to feign excitement and not dampen their joy. My mouth is still shocked closed from our little encounter, so I give them two big thumbs up, heavy bags be darned.

It's going to be a long walk back to the house.

CHAPTER 15

Victorian Face-Palm

»» ———————————— ««

This cannot be happening. I must've had an allergic reaction to the adhesive product used to glue the extra eyes to my forehead. Not even the delicious scents of biscuits and gravy coming from downstairs can distract me from this tragic development. I'm trying not to hog the single upstairs bathroom while everyone hurries to get ready for church, but no amount of face wash can remove these red circles. Talk about getting kicked when you're down.

"Hadley, I hafta pee." Libby bangs on the door in frantic desperation.

"Okay, okay. Sorry." I open the door and her eyes go wide.

"*Gurl.* You're definitely gonna need momma's concealer." The tiny diva sticks her hip out and stares.

"How do you even know what concealer is?" Based on her offended expression, I've insulted her. "Never mind." Shoulders slumped, I skirt around Libby and head off to find Karie.

It's strange standing in their large master bathroom with their toothbrushes and combs scattered around the counter and matching bathrobes hanging from the towel closet door. I feel like an intruder. Karie doesn't seem to notice my unease and hands over a half-empty tube of foundation the second she recovers from taking in the scene that is my face. Unfortunately, her fair complexion is a solid two shades lighter than mine. Must be the ginger genes.

Back in my room, I sit at my desk in front of the small compact mirror from my bag and cake on the makeup. I look positively Victorian. Queen Elizabeth would be proud, but I wish I could crawl back into bed and hide under my pillow until this plague disappears. Church won't wait forever, however, so I soldier on to Sunday School and pretend I don't look like a ghost with measles.

There's no avoiding Franny when I get there, either. "Um, are you ill?" She gapes at my new complexion.

"I'm fine." I shut my eyes and lean my head back against the papasan chair in the far corner of the youth center. "My pride hurts."

"What's wrong? You seemed so excited to take Patrick and Libby trick-or-treating last night."

I suppress a moan and squeeze my eyes even harder. "We had a great time. We ran into Colton and–"

"And Zeke? Isn't he adorable? He is such a sweet kid. Too bad his sister forgot how to be a decent human being." She seems so excited to talk about Zeke. But anyone who lives in the Broadwater equivalent of the Taj Mahal and has Colton wrapped around his finger cannot possibly have it all that bad.

I stare at her, not sure how to barrel through the rest of the story. "Yes. They were with Princess Kyra in her obnoxious castle."

Franny's eyes go so wide I can see the whites and the guttural roar that emanates from her tiny frame is as impressive as it is scary and unexpected. "*What* did you just say?"

"Um, well, when Patrick and Libby knocked on the door of our last house of the night, Kyra answered in a dress fit for Project Runway. She was all smug like, 'Let me get my Prince so he can see how pathetic and ugly you are.' Then Colton, her perfect Prince Charming, struts in with—Zeke, right?—and I guess he's all mad 'cause I'm there, all decked out in my hideous cockroach costume, lookin' like a wreck, and—"

She holds up a hand. "Stop. First, you're rambling. Second, Kyra wasn't part of the deal." She tilts her head, deep in concentration.

"What deal?" I bite my lip and wait.

"Remember when I told you not to ask Colton about the Halloweentown Bag? Zeke, man, he adores Colton, always has. He, Kyra, and Colton have dressed up together for Halloween the last three years and I guess my cousin didn't have it in him to refuse to dress up with him this year, too. Zeke's eight and has cerebral palsy. He's small so he looks a lot younger than he is."

"I don't get why Colton had to be so hush-hush about that?"

"Because Kyra makes him grouchy—he's not himself. Anyway, the deal was, NO Kyra. She's been trying to get back with Colton, but the harder she pushes the more resentful he gets. She tried to guilt him into letting her join their dress up gig and I guess she got her way. Ugh. Of course she did." Franny purses her lips.

I don't have much to add to that, but it seems like Franny isn't finished.

"I bet Colton was livid." She shakes her head.

"Hardly. He wasn't mad. He looked annoyed that I was there." A strangled laugh escapes my throat, despite my best efforts to suppress it. "His smile slipped the moment he recognized me. Like I ruined their perfect evening."

Franny, face all wrinkled up, stares at me as if I've lost my mind. "Hadley, are you serious? You might be the most boy-oblivious person in the history of ever. How is it not obvious to you that—"

Before I can process whatever loaded statement she was about to make, the roar of the speaker system interrupts us. Justin, our youth pastor, grabs a mic to lead us in prayer. Maybe I can grill Franny after church.

###

Following the service, Greg takes us out to eat at his favorite Mexican restaurant. Queso covers a multitude of awkward situations. I was hitting the cheese dip hard, too, until Patrick double-dipped, then triple-dipped, a chip. No, thank you.

This restaurant serves Nonny's favorite soup, *carne de res*, so I place an order to-go and thank the insta-fam for letting me visit her when they drop me off at the nursing home.

"Hi honey, are you visiting with Ms. Dawna this afternoon?" The receptionist recognizes me right away since I visit so much.

"Yes ma'am."

"No boyfriend this time?"

No boyfriend anytime. "Er, no ma'am."

"Well, I know she'll be thrilled to see you. She talks about you all the time."

I knock on Nonny's door but don't hear a response. I slip in anyway, and besides the football game playing softly on the television in the corner, the sterile room is quiet.

I'm hesitant to speak, fearing words would make the time go too quickly, and it hurts to think my precious time with Nonny is running short.

Finally, I break the silence. "Nonny, are you awake?"

Her eyes flutter open and a smile spreads across her face. "What's new with my favorite granddaughter?"

Yep, still Nonny. "I'd be flattered if I weren't your only grandchild."

She chuckles and I pretend I don't notice her wince when she does.

Pulling the table to her bedside, I open her soup from the restaurant. "How are you, Nonny? I've missed you." I give a gentle squeeze to her frail hand, then take a seat in the recliner.

"Just peachy, Hon. Tell me a story about those siblings of yours."

I whip out my phone and show her the pictures from Halloween and one of Libby getting a medal at last week's cross-country race. I've never seen a kid so proud to earn a green fifth place ribbon. Always astute, Nonny asks me to share more about trick-or-treating, so I repeat the entire mortifying story.

Nonny puts a hand to her lips and hums. I appreciate the wisdom evident in her eyes. "Hmmm. There might be more to this story than you know. You should give that boy the benefit of the doubt. Talk to him. You two seemed to get along so well the last time you were here."

That sounds like an awful idea, but it's not like I can avoid him, even if I wanted to. I have a month left of my internship and a giant project to finish. He also lives in my head rent-free, but I'm trying to force an eviction.

"I will try my best to be professional while working with my strictly platonic mentor." I practiced that line in my head, but Nonny purses her lips and gives me a skeptical expression. I think she can see right through me.

"Hadley." Nonny's tone suddenly turns serious.

"Yeah, Nonny?"

She takes a deep breath and pauses, seeming to gather her thoughts.

"It has been a blessing to be your grandmother. I have enjoyed raising you and I always considered it an opportunity to parent for a second time. I might not have deserved that chance, but I thank God every day for it. I got so much satisfaction from watching my grandchild grow, develop new skills, become a woman..."

She looks away and my heart hurts to see her eyes begin to water. "I know you don't want to hear it, but I'm ready to go home, Hadley. I'm ready to be with the Captain again."

"Nonny, stop," I plead, barely a whisper.

"No sugar," she continues, "Philippians 1:21. 'For to me, living means living for Christ, and dying is even better.' I'm ready to go." The tear I try desperately to hold in slides down my face. I swallow the lump in my throat.

"You know what else I'm going to say, right?" She stares at me intently.

"Um, no?"

She smiles. "Yes, you do. God is still good."

"God is still good, Nonny." I know in my heart He is, but my brain keeps questioning his goodness. Why does my Nonny have to suffer?

We sit in silence and watch the game for a few plays. I don't know if Nonny has more deep declarations to make, but I'm content to sit with her in the quiet and watch grown men smash into each other.

"Hadley, honey?"

"Yes, Nonny?" I guess she wasn't done after all.

"What on earth is all over your face?"

Face-palm, it would seem. The dam of tension that had built in my chest releases, and I burst out laughing. Leave it to Nonny to bring a bit of comedic relief.

###

Tuesday afternoon, I swing open the side door to Southern Salvage and I scurry in before it can close, winking at Twinkles as I go. The warm air is so welcoming against the cooling temperatures outside.

"Nice Christmas sweater." Uncle Mike's voice drips with amusement, probably because it's early November.

"Thanks. Now that Halloween season is over, it's socially acceptable to start celebrating Christmas. Christmas music, Christmas sweaters, Christmas everything."

"We Sturgests don't like to skip Thanksgiving here at Southern Salvage." He not-so-subtly directs his gaze to the Christmas display Franny is building in the store-front window. "We like to keep our festive customers happy, both those who deliberately pause to show their thankfulness and those more ungrateful types who skip turkey day altogether."

"Uncle Mike, there were like, four women at the original Thanksgiving, and—

"Somebody had to serve the meal…"

"—and you know what they shared the most at that dinner table? Smallpox. Do you think the Wampanoag were thankful for that?" I ignore his chauvinistic jabs.

Mike smirks. "Calm down, Lucretia Mott. I'm just saying you gotta stop and count your blessings. Gotta be thankful."

"I'm thankful to celebrate Christmas for almost two solid months. Thank-you-very-much. Happy Birthday, Jesus." I bat my eyelashes and offer an exaggerated grin.

He blinks. "I ought to make you decorate a Thanksgiving display just to teach you a lesson."

"Might have to be a small one. Don't you have an election day display to get ready before next week?" I regret it as soon as I say it, sure I've set myself up for another jab.

"Well, I'll be doggone, a woman voting."

Yep, there it is.

"Since 1920, which was over *one hundred years* ago. And don't get too excited, I'm only seventeen."

"Thank goodness. I couldn't figure out how anyone could fit a poll booth in their kitchen." Uncle Mike scratches his head.

"I'm thankful you're kidding." I deadpan.

"Am I, though?" he asks with a wink.

And right up to that point, it was witty rainbows and snarky unicorns. Until…

Until I *felt* Colton's presence like an electric current in the air, like I always do when he's nearby. So much for platonic professionalism. My plan of action: run and hide. Why? Because I'm a coward. In my panic, I make an about-face and run straight into him, face-planting into his chest. It's a bit like headbutting an oak tree and I stumble backwards. Colton offers an awkward, yet distinctly masculine "Oof."

He's holding the hand of the same sweet little boy from trick-or-treating, sitting in a blue motorized wheelchair, legs twisted inward. I've never seen my crush holding a child's hand, but I'd swoon if I weren't still mortified from Saturday's experience.

Mike, however, is a different story. "Zeke—my man. It has been a minute. Let me introduce you to Miss Hadley." Zeke's face lights up when he sees Mike, a grin taking over his angelic face.

Colton clears his throat and looks down at his friend. I cross my arms in the name of self-preservation and take a step back.

"I met Hadley Saturday." Zeke's grin grows even bigger. Apparently, my hideous costume earned me a fan. And thankfully last night's Benadryl removed any last traces of it… I give him a nod and a small wave in response, with one arm this time instead of four. He looks even more excited to meet me than he was to see Mike. Maybe it will be a little easier to pretend I'm not affected by Colton when Zeke's around.

Mike offers him a cosmic brownie from the back and they head off together. Colton takes a step toward me and reaches for my arm. I stiffen, and when I tuck my hands behind my elbows, his shoulders drop.

"Hey." He rubs the back of his neck. "I was hoping we could talk for a minute before you started working on your project. Please."

"Um, I have a lot to do. Maybe we could talk while we work?"

He opens his mouth to say something, but he's interrupted by Zeke's wicked older sister, Kyra. "Zeke? Anyone seen Zeke?"

Welp, off to work for me.

"Don't leave today before we get a chance to discuss something." His jaw does this twitchy thing that makes me nervous. And a little giddy, too.

Kyra starts to sulk over towards us, chin up, so I give Colton a "Yes sir" sandwich and disappear.

Crisis averted, so why am I disappointed?

CHAPTER 16

Let's Taco 'Bout It

≫ ———————————— ≪

I never got to talk to Colton before I left work yesterday, which is on me since I morphed into a stealth-like ninja and avoided him. If I couldn't evade him and it seemed like he might broach the subject of Halloween, I questioned him about how to attach a part to the light. Or took a picture for the store's Instagram feed. Or asked him to explain astrophysics. All necessary, mostly relevant, completely elusive.

Part of me wanted to discuss the trick-or-treating incident in hopes that it was all a terrible misunderstanding and he's actually secretly in love with me. Already spoke to Greg and bought a ring and everything.

Yeah right.

The other half of me is afraid he'll clarify exactly what I suspect—that he's back together with Kyra and so sincerely apologetic that he confused me by staring at my lips and almost kissing me in a non-platonic, non-mentor/mentee moment.

Oops, so sorry, won't happen again. The churning in my stomach would like to have a word.

Wednesday at school offers a great distraction, as our APUSH class is planning the ceremony for next week's Veteran's Day program. We meet in the school's auditorium and the front several rows of the massive room are filled with squirmy children, excited about the change in their daily routine and anxious to work with high schoolers. I spot Zeke in the handicapped space and wave. He grins and returns the gesture.

Mr. Howardson interrupts the chaos. "Good morning, everyone. Settle down please. We are thrilled to have the fourth and fifth-grade classes from Broadwater Elementary join us as we plan for this special program commemorating the sacrifices made by our Veterans, past, present, and future. Each of the four visiting classes have been paired with a trio of my students, while the rest of my students have either been assigned lighting, programs, or acoustics."

I bite my lip as he reads off the lists of assignments, shocked to find I've been paired with Mrs. Lydia Sturgest's fourth grade class.

Lydia Sturgest. As in Colton's mom. I note the exits and try to squelch my desire to flee.

Zeke waves his hands in a wild display of excitement. "Hadley! Hadley, you're with me!"

I shake my hands out as I walk over and take a seat beside him when a gorgeous brunette strides confidently to us. A warm, genuine smile gives her face a glow. "Hadley Edwards? It is a pleasure to meet you. I've heard so many wonderful things." She has? Colton definitely inherited his striking blue eyes and dark hair from his mother. Gaping with a dumbstruck stare probably isn't the best first impression, but here I am.

She gestures to my buddy. "I see you've met Zeke?"

He starts to giggle. "I think Colton likes Hadley."

Oh. My. Gosh.

Help my thundering heart, because she leans down and, in a loud fake-whisper, says, "Me too."

Why doesn't the floor ever open up and swallow me?

"Ignore us," she smiles. "We like to tease. All is fair game with Colton when it comes to Zeke."

It's a good thing I don't have to respond, because I don't think I could if I wanted to.

Instead, I quickly change the subject and get down to work. "Your class is in charge of helping us create a slideshow for the presentation. We need to collect pictures and add music from each branch of the U.S. Military. Think we can make that happen before next Wednesday?"

"We absolutely can, can't we, class?" At Mrs. Sturgest's question, the class gives an enthusiastic variety of positive responses. They're ready, that's for sure. My two classmates and I divide up the group between ourselves as we start to work. One group is assigned to collect pictures from the community, another group works on music, and the last starts adding information to the images we've already received.

"Didn't your dad serve in Vietnam, Mrs. Sturgest? We should add his picture to the slideshow." How awesome would that be to get his photograph?

Mrs. Sturgests nods. "Yes, but he sometimes gets uncomfortable about celebrations or self-promotion. I bet he'd share a picture if you asked him."

Me? Why would she think that?

She points to a pile of photos. "But I understand your grandfather served in the Navy, right? Do you have any photos of him?"

I do. And I can't wait to share this with Nonny.

Our hour with the kids goes by too fast. Time really does fly when you're having fun. We're quick to clean up our work and then Zeke startles me when he rolls over and gives me a giant hug. Before I think more of it, I hug him back. Side-hug Hadley is evolving.

Oof. Pain radiates up from my big toe. I grab my foot as I hobble on one leg. I've been so distracted today and completely failed to notice the thigh-high bronze statue blocking my path. An hours-long, unplanned trip to the hospital with Nonny will do that, I suppose. The statue is completely nude, so I'm not sure how I missed it. Modest is hottest, so I peg-leg it over to the front display, grab one of the Southern Salvage t-shirts, and give the statue some dignity.

"You bring your A-game today, Hadley?" It's Uncle Mike in a booger-green shirt that reads "Want to Taco 'Bout It?" with a giant taco above the words. I do my best to nod and smile, but it's half-hearted. I don't have it in me today. I guess he can tell, because he gives me a quick look of concern, brows raised, then nods and heads off.

I sit down at the Way Maker station and set out my tools.

And here comes the man of the hour, wearing a navy hoodie and faded jeans with sneakers. His top makes his blue eyes stand out. My heart wants to burst through my ribcage.

"Want some help?" Colton offers. I give another half-hearted smile and shake my head to say, "no thanks." He frowns, hesitates, then opens his mouth like he has something to say. He must change his mind, though, because he turns and starts to sort cans of stain.

I get to work cutting the last few bottles and after a while I've got a rhythm going. Tape the bottle, score the cut line, set the bottle in boiling water, then ice water, and repeat until the top breaks away from the bottom. I cut seven in all, like a machine running on autopilot. I can feel Colton watching me, but I'm not interested in chatter even though he keeps attempting to make small talk.

He's persistent, I'll give him that. Mike walks by again. Colton snorts at his shirt then nudges me on the shoulder. "You and I never got to taco 'bout anything the other day. You can't keep avoiding me."

I take a deep breath, thankful I wore my big girl panties today. "Alright. Lettuce taco-bout it." That's as witty as I can get on three hours of restless sleep.

I reach for the rotary tool to even out the glass edges.

Colton gasps.

"Hadley!"

I follow his gaze to find red oozing from my hand. Guess I'm not the focused machine I pretend to be. At least not today.

"Come on, Hads, let's go take a look." Colton grabs my good hand.

But I don't respond. My eyes stay fixed on the fresh gash in my palm. A wave of nausea washes over me and I squeeze my eyes closed to keep the room from spinning.

"*Hadley...*" Colton whispers. He leads me to the staff room. "Take a seat on the counter by the sink." He hoists me up and I lean against the side of the fridge. "Give me a sec to grab the first aid kit. Here, hold this cloth tight." I hear him through a tunnel, like an echo.

When he returns, he gently lifts my chin. "You alright?"

I stare back at him as a single tear makes its way down my cheek. "I don't want to go back to the hospital today."

With his thumb, he wipes away the errant tear. "Is Nonny in the hospital?"

I nod, another tear threatening to spill over.

"Let me take a peek. You might not have to."

He grabs a pair of latex gloves from the kit and pulls them on his hands, even does a goofy "Ohhhh snap" joke when the band slaps against his skin. I appreciate the effort, so I offer a little smile. Colton is so patient and calm–you wouldn't guess that a guy who messes around with power tools all day could be so delicate. He holds the back side of my hand while the hydrogen peroxide washes the red down the drain and tiny white bubbles form a pink foam on the wound.

"I think we should amputate. Chop it off right about here?" Colton drags a soft fingertip along the bottom of my wrist. Hilarious. He's careful as he continues to pat the area dry, only to have blood well up in the wound again. "The first rule of not freaking out is to stop looking at it. How about focusing those beautiful hazel eyes on mine?" My heart hitches in my chest when I look into his eyes. Does he really think my eyes are beautiful? Or is he just trying to distract me? "Keep looking, Hadley." Like that's hard. I bite my bottom lip and try to ignore the pain. He squeezes the cloth tight against my cut once more.

"I hate to say it, but you probably do need to get this stitched up." The corners of his mouth turn down, as if he's the one in pain. "Don't hate the messenger."

Dizziness washes over me once more as Colton puts his hands on my hips to help me slide off the edge of my seat on the counter. It's hard to tell if it's a loss of blood or the warmth of his touch that has left me off balance.

"Mike!" Colton yells. "Come wait with Hadley while I pull the car around to the back entrance." My knees go weak. Colton grabs the back of the rolling desk chair, wraps one arm around my waist, and guides me safely into it.

"Oh, wah wah wah, a girl gets a little paper cut and –" Whatever pseudo-misogynistic jab was about to roll off Mike's tongue dies when he takes in the bloody scene at the sink. His face goes white, and everything in my vision goes black.

###

Everything is foggy, like when one tries to see underwater, sans goggles. I open and shut my eyes until my vision clears and lift my heavy head off…whoever wears a giant Carhartt jacket?

"My bad, Hadley. I had a brief lapse in judgement back at the store." Mike's tone is serious for a change—almost remorseful—and I certainly didn't expect to come to with my head against his shoulder in the back seat of Colton's Jeep. I refuse to apologize for the little puddle of drool on his shoulder. Serves him right.

Colton opens the door and offers his hand, then pulls me into his side to steady me. If this is the 'injured worker' treatment, I should have gotten hurt a long time ago.

"Your dad is on his way to meet us with your insurance card and I'll stay with you the whole time, if that's ok with you. It should only be a few stitches—totally normal to be nervous, but these people put in enough stitches every they could probably create a new wardrobe. You'll be fine."

He guides me to a seat in the waiting room and insists on me sitting when I attempt refusal. If I'm being honest with myself, I miss his warmth when he leaves to sign me in and a sense of relief washes over me the moment he takes the chair beside me and leans close. "If you feel dizzy again, let me know."

"Colton? Hadley?" My dad strides toward us, looking professional in his khaki slacks, crisp white dress shirt, and navy tie. He nods to Colton, takes a clipboard from the receptionist, and claims the chair on my other side. Taking in the blood-stained cloth tied around my hand, he lets out a low whistle. "Let's get these forms filled out so we can get you taken care of." He digs out his wallet, pulls out a card, and mumbles the insurance group ID and policy numbers as he scribbles on the papers. He stops writing, brows furrowed, and clears his throat. "Uh, Hadley, this is a little embarrassing, but your birthday is September…?"

"Seventeenth," I bite out. The throbbing in my hand is making me a little edgy. Colton rubs at the back of the neck and tries to hide a grin.

"Right." A rather pink flush sweeps across his cheeks. "Any allergies, recent surgeries, history of chronic illnesses?"

"No, sir." Nonny would know this information, but I suppose that's not his fault. I press my good palm against my chest, give myself a little massage, and try not to worry about my grandmother a mere three floors up.

"That's good. A peanut allergy sounds tragic. Life would be pretty sad without JIF."

"What?"

"You know I saw peanut butter here once."

Where on earth is this going?

"It had spread itself too thin." He keeps his face completely void of emotion, surprising me, and I laugh, momentarily distracted from my sleep-deprived, suture-dreading induced anxiety. Colton chuckles softly beside me.

Greg bumps my shoulder with his. "I've got a strong arsenal of dad jokes, should you ever need them."

Before I can respond, a nurse calls me to the back. Both my dad and Colton rise to go with me, but I shake my head. I'd love nothing more than to get this over with, sans witnesses. Colton, however, makes his way to the nurse despite my protest.

"Please, ma'am, she can get dizzy. I just—" Colton bites his bottom lip and nods.

"We'll take good care of her, sir." The double doors to the emergency room swing inward and the polite nurse in purple scrubs walks me back where they do, in fact, take good care of me.

One hour, two dad jokes, and five stitches later, we're back at Southern Salvage.

"A couple of Advil and an iced chai and I bet you'll be good as new."

"Thank you." I breathe a sigh of relief and my shoulders come down from my ears. "So how embarrassed should I be that I sliced my hand on a bottle?"

"Are you kidding? It's a rite of passage around here, remember?" He rolls his sleeve up and shows me his faded puffy welt again, silver from healing over. Colton drops his arm, grabs a bottle of water out of the staff fridge and fishes some ibuprofen from the desk. I'm seated on the counter again—someone cleaned it from earlier—and he comes to stand in front of me, giving me his full attention. "Tell me about yesterday."

I blink, it's been an intense afternoon and I'm not sure which part of yesterday he means. "Uh, well, Zeke told me and your mom that you like me." Oh boy. "A little. Maybe." Why couldn't they have sutured my mouth shut?

Colton swallows back a laugh. "Zeke's usually pretty astute, but I like you way more than a little. I guess I should thank my wingman for having the hard conversations for me..." He is not at all embarrassed to say this, a knowing grin on his handsome face.

"But I meant I want you to tell me what's going on with Nonny."

Of course he did.

I exhale a big sigh as I rest my head against the cabinets behind me and check out the bandages on my cut. "Nonny had to go to the emergency room late last night. The nursing home called the house and..." I glance away, blinking back moisture as I try to finish my sentence, "...and anyway, I didn't sleep much last night."

"I'm sorry, Hadley."

"Colton?" My chin trembles and I put my good hand over it, hoping he doesn't notice.

"Yeah?"

"What does hospice do?"

When he takes too long to answer, I look up from inspecting my bandage to find him running his hand down the side of his cheek. "Uh, well…before my grandmother passed away, they stayed with her in the nursing home and helped make sure she was comfortable."

I lean forward into his chest and he wraps an arm around me to rub soothing circles on my back. With the adrenalin from needing stitches starting to wear off, exhaustion began to return with a vengeance. My pain is beyond tears and I can't even cry, but instead press my trembling lips together and offer a silent prayer for strength.

"I'm sorry," I muffle into his shoulder. "I'm just so, so tired."

He straightens so I sit up as well, immediately missing his warmth and the absence of his touch. He looks over his shoulder to the hideous monstrosity that is Old Faithful. "How 'bout a nap?"

"But the soda bottles? I'm supposed to be working. I left a mess, too."

He reaches for my good hand and helps pull me to my feet. "Don't worry about it, we'll just dock your pay by half."

Ha! A true tragedy since I'm an unpaid intern.

He rubs his palm over the top of my hand he continues to hold, and a pained expression takes over his face. "Wait. About what you saw at Halloween..."

"Colton, you don't have to explain—"

"I was only at their house because it was important to me to keep my promise to Zeke. I couldn't let him down, but I didn't mean to give you the impression I was there for anyone else. I'm sorry it looked that way."

Unable to form a response, I merely nod. He squeezes my hand once more, then

gestures for me to follow him as he rests his hand on the small of my back. He guides me to the ratty orange sofa, the dilapidated couch that all of a sudden looks so comfortable and welcoming.

I collapse on Old Faithful, curl into a ball, and close my eyes. Sure enough, the sofa miraculously morphs into a commercial for a mattress made of clouds. The weight of something, a blanket maybe, falls on top of me. I squint one eye open and realize it's Colton's hoodie he was wearing earlier. It smells like him, and I take a deep breath, which unfortunately leads to a less-than-graceful, loud yawn. I ignore Colton's light chuckle, too tired for embarrassment.

The last thing I recall is a soft touch—a strand of stray hair brushed from my face—and my temple tingles from the contact.

When I wake up an hour and a half later, there's a note to check the fridge resting on the coffee table. I find an iced chai tea latte in a Mug Master's to-go cup waiting inside. And as much as I want to swipe Colton's hoodie, that move seems a little too possessive for our "situationship" and way too bold for me. I fold it neatly and place it on the arm of Old Faithful.

"You're quiet as a mouse when you nap, young lady."

I startle at the presence of the large, stoic man behind the massive desk, so much that I almost drop my drink. "Oh! I'm so sorry Mr. Sturgest. I–I'm not a slacker. It's just, I spent most of last night at the hospital. Ugh, sorry. I don't mean to make excuses. I–"

"It's fine, Hadley. I'm sorry Mrs. Dawna is sick. Colton told me about your cut. Let's have a look at that hand." His deep voice quiets my anxious thoughts and kindness lurks behind the harsh lines surrounding his eyes. He reminds me so much of my grandfather, the Captain. I take a seat on the rolling chair beside his desk and stick my arm out. Calloused, wrinkled hands, strong with age, turn my palm up as he looks through his glasses at the doctor's handiwork. "Not bad. You keep that clean and make sure to put plenty of Vaseline on it."

"Yes sir."

"Have a good night, Hadley."

"Thank you, you too." But as I stand and turn to leave, I remember what Colton's mom said. "Mr. Sturgest?"

He lifts a brow.

"May I borrow a picture of you in your military garb for our Veteran's Day Assembly?"

He runs his hand down his beard in contemplation and stares so long, I'm sure he's going to say no. But then he rises from his chair and shuffles through a filing cabinet, pulling out an eight-by-ten sepia copy of him in his dress blues next to a striking young woman.

I study the picture. "Was this your wife? Colton always speaks so highly of his grandmother."

"That's my Carol." He squeezes my shoulder, then points to the photograph. "Make sure I get that back."

"Yes sir. And thank you."

With care, I tuck the photo in my binder before leaving. I sip my drink the entire walk home, savoring it and thoughts of Colton on the way.

CHAPTER 17

Hadley Gets EMOTAL

»» ——————————— «

EMOTE + SPIRAL
EMOTAL
|i'mōdəl|
v. to feel, think, and judge oneself in rapid succession,
ultimately causing immobility.
-The Emotionary: A Dictionary of Words that Don't Exist
for Feelings That Do, page 6.

"Wow, that's a lot of hearts." Raven nudges me
playfully.

I pause, lift my pastel oil crayon, and stare at her. I'm
sandwiched between Raven and Ashley in art and they're
both looking at me funny. "Did you say something?" I can
barely finish my artwork anyway, with this bandage on my
hand.

"Oh, oh wow. You've got it bad." Raven taps her finger
on the edge of one particularly cute pair of tiny hearts.

When I try and fail to bite back a grin, her face lights
up. "Eeeeeek, it's your situationship, isn't it? Tell me, tell
me, tell me."

"*Shhhhhhhh,*" I hiss, embarrassed. "Colton told me
that he likes me."

"Like, *likes* you, likes you?" When I nod, Raven squeals, but Mr. Moses' very un-Bob Ross-like frown warns us to quiet down. I have a little moment of déjà vu as I repeat the same conversation Taylor and I had when we Facetimed last night. Libby overheard a bit of my gushing and made a gag face before running out of my room.

"That was a lot of likes, but yeah, he did. It's just…"

Ashley holds up a hand to cut me off. "Oh my gosh, it's just what? What could you possibly question about dating Colton Sturgest?"

"Well, it isn't necessarily the possibility of dating Colton, it's that I've never really dated… *ever.*"

"Never?" Raven scrunches her nose. "You went on a date with Peter, didn't you?"

"I went on half a date with Peter, and that's different. If that counts as a date, I've been on a ton." Ashley raises her brows like she wants more details, but I know they'd both be disappointed in my lackluster serial double-dating adventures.

"You've never had a serious boyfriend?" Raven asks.

It's more of a statement than a question, but I answer anyway. "I've never had a boyfriend, period."

"Yet." She wiggles her eyebrows at me and my cheeks warm. "But why not?" Raven's squeal attracted the attention of our neighbors, some are even whispering or leaning in closer to listen. I'm a little uncomfortable with the scrutiny of our overly curious classmates.

"Daddy issues?" Ashley pipes in.

I snort, which doesn't help divert the nosy glances. "I met 'daddy' about three and a half months ago, so that's a giant no."

Ashley and Raven exchange a glance.

"Mommy issues?" Ashley needs to major in psychology when she goes to college next year.

I stare at them. "No? She left when I was really young. Nonny raised me until we moved here." I'm starting to sound like Little Orphan Annie, and I don't like it.

"Let's play worst-case scenario."

Ashley nods in response to Raven's suggestion.

"Yes, let's. Sounds morbid and counterproductive." Elbow on the desk, I rest my temple on my good palm and surrender.

"What's the absolute worst thing that could happen if you went out with Colton?" Raven asks.

"First of all, Colton hasn't asked me out. Second, *so* many things. I could sweat through my shirt and make him toss his cookies. I could have stank nasty gas and he'd never speak to me again. I could snort while eating spaghetti and a noodle could fly out of my nose. I could have a cliff-diver dangling from my nose… in, out, in out. I could—"

"Stop." Raven holds a hand up. "You need to lighten up big time. Have any of these actually come close to happening on any of your dates?"

"Of course not, but you said worst case, so I went for it." What was I supposed to do?

Raven rolls her eyes. "What is a realistic worst-case scenario?"

The mathematician in me would like to point out that while those are all improbable, they're not impossible, but I consider her question. "He might get to know me and not like me, which would sting. I could fall head-over-heels in love, but he doesn't, crushing my heart. My Nonny is about to die, and I just moved hundreds of miles to a new family, new school, new everything, and he might not want to deal with that emotional train wreck, all of which would stink because I really like him, too."

My mini outburst is met by dead silence. On the other side of the room, someone scuffs a shoe against a chair, and I realize all eyes are on me. When I look at Ashley, she's tearing up.

"I guess Daddy issues might have been easier, huh?" I shrink into myself and put my chin down.

"Girl, no. You go for it. Colton is lucky a girl like you is into him." Raven reaches for my good hand and gives a healthy squeeze.

"Slay Queen. Slay allllll day." A random kid a few rows back cheers and murmurs of agreement sprinkle the room. How did this turn into a mini pep-talk? *So* glad everyone knows my business now.

I'm touched by their support and hope my brain can get in sync with my heart. Most boys are scary, but Colton? He's the good kind of scary. Scary exciting. Maybe I do need Ashley to psychoanalyze me on a giant couch in a therapist's office.

That night, after church and my run with Libby, I shower and settle in to tackle some homework. I've added and edited almost all the Veteran's Day pictures collected by the kids and submitted by various community members. All except for Mr. Sturgests' and the one of Nonny and the Captain.

All the Veterans' pictures are special, but these two are extra special to me. I lay them flat on my desk, side by side, and admire them. I don't understand why or how I've earned a soft spot in Mr. Sturgests' heart, but he seems like a kindred spirit, so similar to my grandfather. I've somehow managed to endear myself to him and that comforts me.

And the Captain in his Navy blues, standing next to a younger version of my Nonny… it pulls at the heartstrings.

I think about my response to the Naval Lab's internship offer and hope my choice would've made him proud. I'm still not confident enough to tell anyone but Nonny about my decision, one that plagued me for weeks. But November first wouldn't wait for me, so I prayed for discernment and went with my gut. The peace I felt after I mailed the response confirmed I'd made the right choice. But I'm not ready to tell Taylor my decision. Or Libby. Or Colton. Or... anyone who isn't Jesus, to be honest.

###

Twenty-five ceiling swirl patterns multiplied by thirty-two ceiling swirl patterns equals eight hundred ceiling swirl patterns, which confirms my earlier manual count. I counted the squares on my quilt and the slats in the Venetian blinds, too. Sheep didn't help, those rude little rams. Sleep is elusive. When I called Nonny earlier to tell her goodnight, she sounded so weak. It was the shortest conversation we've had since we moved to Kentucky. When I consider flipping the light on and reading a book, my phone buzzes.

Hey. We should celebrate your progress on the light tomorrow. Can I take you out to dinner?

Nom nom nom FOOD! But... who is this?

Colton. I guess you probably do get asked out a lot, huh?

What memes would pop up if I searched "flattered and panicked"? I start to type a response at least four times but hit the backspace button. Nothing I can think of is cute, witty, or confident enough. I hate that he can see those indecisive gray bubbles on his screen.

How about a practice date? I can pick something up and we can share it in the staff room.

Potassium.

Huh?

I mean "K." K is the atomic symbol for Potassium. Welp, I've blown it now.

Dang, Hadley, you are a nerd. What's your favorite food?

I'm not picky. Surprise me.

Potassium.

Forget the book, I'm not sleeping tonight.

###

Colton plops two giant to-go bags from "El Restaurante Increíble" on the staff-room counter and, oh my, it smells delicious. "I ordered us Mexican, and you're in for a treat."

"First of all, you can't go wrong with Mexican. More importantly, what's the treat?" I lean in to take a peek at the grease-stained bags.

"Fish tacos." His voice drips with reverence.

"Apparently, you can go wrong with Mexican." I deadpan and frown. "That sounds like vomit in a tortilla."

He places a hand on his chest, feigning offense, then clears off a space on a side table he's creating from reclaimed barn wood.

I notice the tag with the description of the piece, its provenance, and Southern Salvage's hallmark verse. "2 Corinthians 5:17. Nice. The new creation concept really ties in with the whole Southern Salvage theme."

"You okay today, Hadley?" Colton asks, brows furrowed. "Other than comparing tacos to hurl, you've been pretty quiet. Hardly made a peep when you were working on the light."

"You're welcome." I attempt to joke, and to my delight he gives a soft chuckle. He's quite a moment, and I realize he's waiting on me to respond. I hesitate, then ask, "Have you ever... I just…"

Inhale. Exhale. Deep breath.

"Lately, I've been a little lost. Where do I belong, why is everything happening, who am I? I'm scared that I'm an unwanted inconvenience, but at the same time I really enjoy it here. I *like* my insta-family. And the fear of the unknown can sometimes get overwhelming. Do those fears make me a bad Christian?"

Colton's eyes go wide and his mouth slackens, like maybe he wants to say something. Before he can, I continue rambling, almost like I can't stop driving this hot mess express.

"I mean, I *worry* about how much I *worry,* and I don't want God to be mad at me or disappointed with me." I'm fidgeting with my necklace now. "Like, how dumb is this? One of my fears is that I secretly get on everyone's nerves but the people I choose to hang out with are too nice to tell me."

He raises a brow and grins.

My mouth goes dry, but I want to trust Colton. "I've felt far from God since Nonny's *big news,* but I'm starting to see that these experiences could be bringing me closer to Him?"

Colton sets down his taco and wipes his hands on a napkin. He seems to think about what he wants to say while he finishes chewing his food. "God's big enough for our questions. Maybe his answers will bring you some peace."

Well, alrighty.

"Romans 8:28." Colton says this with so much confidence, I feel it too. "And we know that in all things God works for the good of those who love him, who have been called according to his purpose."

There's nothing I can say to this, so I process it in silence.

"You really think you're some kind of inconvenience? Like you're broken and not worthy to be here, or something crazy like that?" Colton stares at me.

I blink, unsure if his question is rhetorical or not.

"That's nonsense." He points to his Styrofoam container. "These taco shells are broken, and if you don't think I'm happy to have them in my life you're seriously mistaken." My face warms at the double meaning, and I bask in his compliment.

From that point, we eat and we flirt, and I have zero complaints in my life. Every once in a while, our hands graze the other's and those little zings of electricity become addictive. They go nicely with chips and queso.

Until…

Until Mike barges in.

"Hadley," he says, no nickname or dig this time, which scares me. "Your stepmom is here. I got your backpack for you." Colton stands and steps toward me, the concern etched on his face evident. I swallow the lump in my throat and let Mike help me with the pack straps. Colton walks me to the door and nods to Karie, whom I can tell by her flushed face and red eyes has been crying.

"Karie?"

She swallows me in a hug. "Your Nonny is asking for you Hun. She's had a hard day."

Tears well up in my eyes and I bite my lip in hopes they won't spill over.

It's a quiet ride to the hospital. My feet heavy, I walk down the sterile, white halls and head for her room. When I enter, the atmosphere is somber, and everyone is quiet. Nonny appears so small in her bed when I pull a chair up beside her. I reach for her frail hand. I thought she was asleep, but she gives my fingers a soft squeeze. She's so feeble I'm afraid to squeeze it back.

"Nonny?" I choke out. I take a deep breath and try to calm myself. "Nonny. It's me, Hadley."

"Of course I know it's you dear," she says slowly and smiles. "Hadley, dear, I'm glad you came. I'm ready to go home and I want to tell you goodbye."

My eyes water. I hate this.

"Remember Hadley, God is still good."

I want to converse with her, but words fail me, so I apply soft pressure to my grasp so she knows I'm with her and I'm following what she's saying. I swallow and blink away my tears.

"I love you, Hadley."

"I love you, too, Nonny." I say it twice, louder and with confidence the second time so I know she hears me. "You can go home, Nonny, I know I'll get to see you again. I love you, too. I love you, too."

Nonny falls asleep. I sit in the chair with her until the sun goes down. Around 8:30, Nonny stirs in her sleep and I watch as her chest rises and falls. And then, gently, her chest doesn't rise again. I choke back a sob as Karie wraps her arms around me. I bury my face in her shoulder and ugly cry. I don't know how long I sob until my tears run out and give way to silence. Nurses enter Nonny's room and Karie suggests we leave them to their task.

I kiss Nonny's forehead one last time and whisper, "Goodbye, Nonny."

CHAPTER 18

Teddy's Light

»» ———————— ««

It is well known that President Theodore Roosevelt kept a diary. On February 14, 1884, Teddy lost his mother and young wife within hours of one another. His entry for that fateful Thursday said only this:

"The light has gone out of my life."

I know how Teddy felt.

God is still good.

CHAPTER 19

Funerals Are for the Living

»» ———————————— ««

Nothing.

I feel… *nothing.* Just numb.

That's not true. I feel tired. Friday mornings are supposed to be happy, filled with excitement over the upcoming weekend. But right now, I'm lying listless in my bed, staring at the pictures Libby colored and hung on my corkboard. Hard to see in the dark of five a.m., but I can still make out the image of our stick figures running together.

My alarm isn't set to go off for a few more hours. When your primary parental figure has visitation and a funeral scheduled, you get a free pass from high school.

I wade through the rest of the day in a groggy, empty version of myself. I have exactly two things I need to do–send the final Veteran's Day Slideshow to Mr. Howardson and Mrs. Sturgest, and sit down with the funeral home director, Greg, and Karie to plan Nonny's service. The first is easy, the second, not so much. Why are there so many details in a funeral? And the paperwork that comes with passing away… I'm going to plant a tree when this is over to appease my guilty conscience. Maybe two trees.

I don't know where the time went today, but I can almost hear Nonny's favorite soap opera theme *"... like sands through the hourglass..."* It's like I just woke up, but Libby and Patrick are already putting on their pajamas and discussing which books to choose for their bedtime stories.

"Hadley might need a night off, guys." Karie's hushed words still manage to seep down the hall and make their way to my room, even with the door closed. "Mommy and Daddy are going to tuck you in this evening."

"But–" Patrick's tiny voice interrupts.

"No buts. Off to brush your teeth, little man. Patrick Kendall, where are you going?"

My door swings open and Patrick marches over to my desk in green Ninja Turtle pajamas. He wraps his small arms around my waist, buries his still-damp hair into my side, and muffles, "Night night, sissy. I wuv you." Startled by his unusual display of brotherly affection, I recover and give him a squeeze. As quickly as he rushed in, he leaves. But what a gift that brought to my aching heart.

###

Saturday morning, after another restless night, even the smell of the baking Dutch baby from downstairs can't help me rally to face the day. My phone buzzes from my desk, but I ignore it. When it buzzes again, I reach over and reluctantly check the caller, then accept the Facetime request from Taylor. Even when it's evident she's been crying, her face flushed and eyes bloodshot–she's still strikingly beautiful. She speaks first, "Hey stranger. Long time no see."

"Taylor, what's going on?" She's in the passenger's seat of Colton's Jeep. Franny waves from the backseat.

"My plane just landed. I flew in for the services and Colton and Franny picked me up."

That just makes me tear up all over again. I'm desperate for her friendship right now and I don't know how they arranged this, but gratitude fills my chest, momentarily eclipsing the heavy weight of grief.

"Oh, Hadley." Her eyes fill with tears. "I'm not used to seeing my bestie bawling. I'm sorry."

"You don't have anything to be sorry for," I choke out. "I'm just so happy you're able to make it." I raise my voice a little so her car companions can hear me. "Thank you for picking up Taylor."

"No, I mean, I'm so glad I'm coming too, but I meant I'm sorry about Nonny." Words fail me, so I give a simple nod and turn my head away from the screen, too afraid that if I look at her, I'll start crying and won't be able to stop.

Again.

"We're stuck in a little traffic jam, but once everything clears, we should be at your house in about an hour." Franny has the phone turned to focus on Colton, clad in a blue Kentucky basketball hoodie and some afternoon stubble.

Taylor turns the phone back to herself and winks. "You've got yourself a very sweet guy here, Hads."

Oh my gosh, she called him 'my guy,' essentially giving him a label. At least I can always count on her to provide a goofy distraction. Franny is cheesing in response to the name Taylor's gifted him, but there's no objection from Colton.

"I think you're right. Love you, Taylor."

"Love you too."

I click the red button to end the call, then lay my head back on the pillow and stare at my ceiling. There's no telling how much time passes while I zone out, could be five minutes, could be five hours. A knock at the door interrupts my melancholy.

"Hadley, mommy said we should go for a run." It's Libby on the other side of the door, and she's entirely too cheery.

"What?"

"She said it will make you have informants."

No clue what that means, but hard pass. I roll over and pretend I can't hear. She doesn't take the hint. The door flies open. She flips on the light, marches over to my bed, and tugs my arm. Libby's surprisingly strong for an eight-year-old.

"Mommy said I mean endorphins. Runnin' will boost them up. They're 'sposed make you happy."

There aren't enough endorphins on this planet to make me forget my Nonny is gone. Still, I get out of bed and shoo her out to get dressed. With tremendous effort, I work through the sludge in my bones to drag on leggings, a sports bra, a long sleeve dry-fit shirt, and my running shoes, not bothering to check if anything matches. I brush my teeth, throw my hair in a bun, have mercy on Libby and roll on some deodorant, and then go search for the insta-sis.

"Wait!" I'm intercepted by Karie, who insists I eat something and hands me a glass of water. A wave of nausea passes over me, but I sip some from the cup to appease her. The sausage link is a true test of my queasiness tolerance, but I soldier through two whole bites to expedite my escape.

"Atta girl." She pats me on the back as she starts walks off, dropping the food issue.

"Karie?" I stop her.

"Yes?"

"Taylor just called from the airport. Thank you for arranging for her to come."

"You can thank your dad—it was all his idea." Oh wow. "And Colton, he helped too." Oh *wow*.

I shuffle back a step. "He did?" My voice sounds soft to my own ears.

A small, knowing grin lights her face as she shakes her head. "Sure did. Don't you have a run to go on?"

Right.

Libby and I, we run. Or try to run, anyway. We make it a full mile before the waterworks start. We slow to a walk and finally, I plop down on a bench beneath a sturdy oak outside of Mug Masters, defeated, and I can't keep it together. Even for my sweet, innocent, spunky little half-sis. The faucet is on and it won't stop.

Somehow, Libby is unfazed. "Momma told me this might happen. It's ok, Hadley. You can cry." Her kindness opens another lock on the dam. So many tears. She sits beside me and rests her head on my shoulder. A solid ten minutes tick by and we sit there in silence. Then, I quit crying, spent. Kind of nice to get it out.

"Um, excuse me. Hadley?" Libby lifts her head and I turn to look over my shoulder at Kyra.

"Hi." I sniffle, embarrassed, knowing I probably resemble a splotchy tomato.

"I'm sorry about your grandmother. You told me once she loved the cranberry scones, so…" She holds out a white paper Mug Master's bag and shrugs. "In honor of Nonny."

"Thank you." I wipe away another tear with the palm of my hand and take the bag from her, grateful when she smiles and nods, staring at the ground as she does. "That's very kind of you."

"See you guys later." Kyra heads back into the store, the little bell above the door ringing as she does.

Well, that was unexpected.

Libby holds my hand as we walk back, her small palm in mine. I shower until the hot water runs cold, eat a massive slice of Dutch baby, then fall asleep for a solid two hours, only waking to get ready for Nonny's visitation.

Visitations are kind of weird. Colton is waiting in the receiving line with a large Southern Salvage bag, which piques my curiosity. I noticed him as soon as he entered and got in line to sign the guest book. He looks handsome in his khaki pants and buttoned dress shirt. The blue of the fabric matches his eyes. He smiles and my weak heart flutters. Even Kübler-Ross' five stages of grief I learned about in psychology class can't compete with crush-induced butterflies. Thankfully, I'm pretty sure Nonny would approve.

I shake hands and hug the strangers in line, but there are a few familiar faces. I stand a little straighter when I spot Taylor in line behind Franny and Colton. Apparently, the traffic jam was a little worse than they thought. When Colton reaches the front of the line, he pulls Twinkles out of the bag and stands her on the chair next to me. I shake my head, confused.

"I didn't want you to have to stand here by yourself. I notice you, Hadley." He taps his pointer finger to his temple. "I know you have some quirky bond with this gnome."

Greg and Karie are sitting in the first row for moral support, but I don't mention that. "Twinkles." I smile, the first one all day.

"Excuse me?"

"Her name is Twinkles. She's not your average gnome."

"Of course not."

"That's a lovely dress you've got her in." I admire her red and white striped doll dress with cute blue stars around the collar and hem of the skirt.

"Her fit is fire, right? Franny's idea. She remembered Nonny loved the Navy, and black is too depressing, so we hooked her up with this drippy, new patriotic ensemble." He grins and I can tell he's proud of himself.

"Well, thanks, I appreciate you bringing her. I was getting a little lonely up here, just me and Nonny."

"Twinkles is more *here* than Nonny, Hadley."

I bite my lip as my chest tightens because Colton's unexpected words sting.

"No, Hadley, no." He squeezes his blue eyes tight and tries again. "What I mean is…visitations and funerals–er, Nonny's funeral–they're supposed to honor her by giving you the opportunity to reflect on your memories together. It should help you acknowledge that she's passed away and you can grieve."

I press my trembling lips together.

Colton gestures to the casket. "Nonny isn't here, Hadley," he whispers. "Funerals are for the living. Not to make you crazy jealous or whatever, but she's with Jesus." He reaches out to grab my hand and gives it a light squeeze.

Oh. *Oh!*

Is it a sin to be jealous of Jesus? Or jealous of Nonny for being with Jesus?

"And with your grandfather." He gives my hand a second squeeze and offers a half grin.

That makes me smile and I squeeze his hand back. He kisses my cheek and moves to the photos displayed of Nonny with various family members. I can feel Greg staring at me from the first row, but I ignore his curious, probing eyes. I'm having a moment with my gnome.

"*M-A-R-R-Y-H-I-M.*" Taylor mouths as she steps up.

"*S-E-V-E-N-T-E-E-N.*" I mouth back. When she rolls her eyes, I mock roll mine back. "Man, I thought it was bad when you constantly tried to set me up on dates. Now you're trying to get me hitched?"

"I get the impression you don't need me as your matchmaker anymore." She feigns a dramatic sigh.

"But I'll always want you as my best-friend." So much for not needing any tissues. With that, we bear hug. It's a hug so tight, I almost fall over. So does Twinkles, but luckily, we both stay on our feet.

The thought that Nonny is no longer in pain *and* she's with Jesus is incredibly reassuring. So is having Taylor here. Twinkles and I tackle the rest of the visitation line as the day passes in a blur.

I fidget with the soft yarn on the end of the heather green Afghan Nonny crocheted when I was in fifth grade, rubbing the cotton fibers between my fingers. It's draped over the beige La-Z-Boy in my living room in Annapolis. Directly across from me, Nonny sits next to the Captain on the matching loveseat, holding hands. They're both wearing such genuine smiles that their faces seem to glow,

221

radiating happiness. Behind them hang framed photographs, one with me, the Captain and Nonny, and a second with me and the Kendalls. Oddly, neither seems out of place, like they've both been hanging there forever.

"What's going on? H-how am I here?" But they don't answer.

Nonny leans in and kisses my grandfather on his cheek. He reaches over and cups my face. "We're both so proud of you, kiddo."

They stand and walk over to the next room, and I follow, the hardwood floors creaking in their familiar way. I'd follow them anywhere. Nonny reaches over to flip the light on in the kitchen, but when a blinding brightness envelopes the room, I turn to see why, only to find myself at the Waymaker station in Southern Salvage. Colton is there, sandwiched between Nonny and the Captain. He's smiling shyly, as the soda bottle fixture I've been working on hangs, completely finished, from the ceiling. It fills the room with warm light.

The Captain speaks now, the timbre of his deep voice causing my skin to tingle. I've missed him so much. "'For I know the plans I have for you,' declares the LORD, 'plans to prosper you and not to harm you, plans to give you hope and a future.'"

Nonny and Colton nod in agreement to my grandfather's declaration.

"Finish the good work you've started, Hadley. We're rooting for you."

I reach out to hug him, then...

I sit up suddenly, taking sharp, deep breaths, gasping for air. My pajama top is drenched in sweat.

Breathe, Hadley.

Breathe.

It was all a dream. An incredibly realistic, tragically beautiful dream.

###

Sunday morning, I rub the sleep from my eyes to find Taylor scrolling through her phone. When she notices I'm awake, she rolls my way and shares her screen with me. It's the Southern Salvage Instagram feed and they've posted a beautiful tribute to Nonny. In the image, a tea light candle burns in one of the bottles I cut. The simple caption reads, "We remember Dawna Edwards as a gentle soul who brightened our lives. John 1:5." It's beautiful.

After church, lunch, and a short existential crisis, we attend the funeral. Sunday was Nonny's favorite day of the week, so we opted for this afternoon instead of postponing it until a weekday. The service is lovely, as was the dinner our church served me and the Kendalls afterwards. Colton was right. Funerals are for the living. They buried my grandfather in a Veterans Cemetery, and this summer I plan to take Nonny's urn to Maryland to be buried with him. I even worked out a way to stay with Taylor before she had to fly back.

Our church isn't far from the Kendall house, so I ask Karie if I can walk home, not entirely alone, since Twinkles will be with me.

I take my time while I stroll and notice flyers for the Broadwater Fall Festival in many of the store window fronts. There is a huge poster-sized flier on the door of Mug Masters, just below an ad for the Kentucky Historical Society. They're at gas-stations, business offices, and the door of the community center. The Captain was right–I need to finish the good work I started, and Nonny always told me anything worth doing was worth doing right. As anxious as I am to buckle down and get the fixture finished, I know I won't rush too much... more time at Southern Salvage means more time with Colton, after all.

But first, I have an early family Thanksgiving with Karie's parents. This will be my first major holiday with the Kendalls and without Nonny. I hug Twinkles against my chest and continue home.

CHAPTER 20

Veteran's, Interns, & Cho's, Oh My!

»» ———————————— ««

Greg and Karie were torn about my decision to return to school today, but I convinced them it would keep me busy, and I also don't want to miss the Veteran's Day Assembly. Nonny's jewelry is stored in my room, and I pick the perfect vintage flag pin to wear on my navy sweater dress. Paired with some cozy leggings and ankle boots, I style my hair in a braided headband and grab my backpack.

The ceremony begins with the presentation of colors, the recitation of the Pledge of Allegiance, and the singing of the national anthem by the BHS choir. I sit, numbly, throughout the speeches and performances but snap out of it as the first notes of "America the Beautiful" begin to play. This needs to be perfect. The slideshow starts and I wiggle in my seat to sit up. I'm proud of the work Zeke, his classmates, and I have put into this, but I'm even more proud of the images of the veterans and their families in the photographs. Especially touching are the images of veterans reuniting with loved ones and friends, highlighting the emotional moments of homecoming. I look around to gauge the reaction of my peers and the other audience members. There isn't a dry eye in the house, so at least I'm not weeping alone. I grin in satisfaction as the final pictures fill the screen–first, the one of Mr. Sturgest and, finally, the one of the Captain with Nonny. I pull in a deep breath and peek at Zeke, who claps wildly as the screen goes dark. I relax in my seat and exhale a sigh of relief.

A moment of silence follows, and I do my best to tame the sounds of my sniffles. Finally, the Veterans in attendance stand to be recognized. When Mr. Sturgest rises, I can hardly believe it–he actually came. Mike, Franny, and Colton are seated beside him, beaming. My heart is so full it could almost burst with gratitude. I can't wait to see all of them at Southern Salvage later.

Colton turns and scans the crowd, eyes landing on me. When I grin and give a little wave, he winks. Thank goodness for these long sleeves — goosebumps have sprung up all over my arms.

As we filter out of the auditorium, Mr. Howardson pulls me aside. "Miss Edwards, I'd like to introduce you to my son-in-law, Matthew." Matthew shakes hands like he's holding a dead fish, but he has a warm smile.

"Nice to meet you, sir." Minus the handshake, anyway.

"You as well. I wanted to compliment you on your presentation, that was quality work, young lady."

"Thank you, sir." Aw, shucks.

"Matthew is chair of the Children's department at the Kentucky Historical Society. I'm not sure if he's more impressed with the presentation or the fact that efficiently and effectively worked with a large group of third graders to create it."

"Both," he grins at me. "Have a lovely Veteran's Day, Hadley."

Huh. How kind.

Mr. Sturgest lets me adjust my internship schedule after missing a few days last week and I'll be out of town Saturday to meet Karie's parents. Some sort of special, pre-Thanksgiving meal. I'm already anxious about having missed so much school and definitely don't want to get behind on the light. If I don't stop biting my fingernails, I won't have any left. The Fall Festival is two weeks away, right after Thanksgiving. Must. Not. Panic. I'm working today, Tuesday, Wednesday before church, and Thursday night to make sure I'm ready. Gonna be a full week.

I'm nervous that things will be weird since losing Nonny between now and the last time I worked. I don't want anyone to treat me like I'm fragile or might break. To avoid any feelings of awkwardness, I decide to bring Twinkles with me to Southern Salvage. Mike slaps a store name tag on her dress that reads "Twinkles: Supervisor" and we plant her at the Waymaker Station like a scarecrow in a field. He's changed from his more formal assembly attire to a dark brown Thanksgiving shirt with a turkey riding a T-Rex. It's weird and funky and I kind of want to ask if it's available in my size. Or not, 'cause Karie's parents may not appreciate such a goofy first impression.

Back to the light fixture. "How are we supposed to transport this to the barn at the fairgrounds? It's huge." I gaze at the still incomplete bottle chandelier.

"And very heavy," Franny adds, wide eyed.

Colton has his arms crossed over his "Judah and the Lion" hoodie, lips pressed together as he considers the question. "We'll need to complete the light to make sure everything is in working order, deconstruct it, transport it, and reconstruct it at the barn."

"Whoa. Won't that be a lot of work?"

"Nah. We got this." He fist-bumps my shoulder and my arm tingles, not because it hurt, but because, hello, it's Colton.

"Are you guys sure you don't mind helping me do all that?" In all seriousness, it looks like a massive undertaking.

"I'm looking forward to it." He offers me an unabashed smile and I get lost in his dimple for a moment.

"Ew. Excuse me while I go talk to Ralph on the big white telephone." Franny rolls her eyes as she says it, but her smile tells me she approves.

Colton and I plunk down on the floor and get to work. For a solid hour, we tackle our task to assemble all 149 precut and sanded bottles and connect them to fireproof sockets. We cut wires, test bulbs, and make a giant mess.

Click.

Franny grins from the other side of the camera. "Oh, this is glorious, organized chaos. Definitely gonna post this on Insta."

While I shrink and pray I don't spontaneously combust—my face hot from embarrassment—Colton reminds her to endorse Bluegrass Bottlers and Southern Salvage. I'll be glad to finally post a picture of the finished project.

I lean forward to hop up and stretch my back, aching from sitting so awkwardly on the concrete. "I'll be right back to help clean up, but is Mr. Strugest here this afternoon?"

"Which one?" Colton asks, not even kidding.

"Your grandfather. I have his picture to give back and I wanted to thank him for attending the ceremony." I play with my hangnail, a little edgy about meeting with him.

"Should be. Check the staff room."

I approach the larger than average door and knock timidly.

"Door's open." Mr. Sturgest's rough, deep voice grants me permission to come in.

"Hi Mr. Sturgest. I wanted to return your photograph and thank you for coming to the Veteran's Day Assembly this morning." I lay a large manilla folder with his picture on his desk.

"My pleasure. Thank you for the invitation." He taps his pen on the yellow pad he's working on.

"Okay, well, thank you again." I guess he's a man of few words, so I turn to see myself out.

"Hadley, one moment, please."

I freeze and turn back to face the patriarch of Southern Salvage.

"Why don't you sit for a bit."

"Yes sir." He's just like the Captain, I remind myself. Nothing to worry about.

He takes a deep breath then makes eye contact. I can see why other people are intimidated. He's stoic, contemplative, and a little rough around the edges.

He clears his throat and begins. "Colton... he's always had this, this *light*, and for the past year, I watched it dim. It killed me inside to watch him self-destruct. He started to shut down. I had almost given up, but I changed the way I was praying. I thought I could fix him myself, shake some sense back into him. But then I just… surrendered. It felt bigger than me and I asked God to fix him or bless him with a friend who could help."

He leans forward in his chair, and I swallow the lump in my throat. "Hadley, I want you to know that Mr. Howardson called me *the next day–"* he points a finger at the phone, as animated as I've ever seen him, "about signing you on as an intern. I don't think it's any big secret I haven't always been a huge fan of the whole internship program, but I'm glad I said yes this time." Mr. Sturgest chokes up and I have to look away to prevent myself from doing the same. He's destroyed my preconceived notion that he isn't a big talker.

He gathers himself and continues. "You're special to us here at Southern Salvage, Hadley. I know you've had a rough year, and I'm glad you and Colton have each other to lean on."

"Me too," I say, but it comes out as a whisper. I see a small smile on Mr. Sturgests' face, but it's fleeting as he spies the store's security cameras and notices the trainwreck that is my work site.

He stands then and says, "Well, that mess won't clean itself, young lady."

And he's back.

"Yes sir." He doesn't have to tell me twice.

###

The rest of this week is more of the same. Go to school, run with Libby, work on the light at Southern Salvage, flirt with Colton. Add in FaceTime with Taylor and I stay so busy–the week flies by.

Early on Friday morning, the sun barely cresting the horizon, we pack up the swagger wagon. Libby has the zoomies in her seat, giddy about visiting NayNay and YeYa's house. She has the absolute weirdest names for grandparents I've ever heard in my life. I thought "Nonny" and the "Captain" were unusual, but these take the cake.

"How did you guys come up with such–*er*–unique names?" I ask Karie as I hand her my bag. She stuffs it in the back of the van with a grunt.

She gives me a funny look and raises her eyebrows. "My nieces couldn't pronounce năinai or yéye when they were toddlers, so NayNay and YeYa sort of stuck. The names trickled down to the rest of the grandchildren." She shrugs like she didn't just pronounce the terms in perfect Chinese, and I freeze, impressed but confused. Karie smiles at my lack of understanding. "My parents are from China. My maiden name is Cho."

I remain frozen as I consider Karie's auburn hair, freckled complexion, and hazel eyes. Yep, still confused.

"That's why we're missing a day of school and celebrating Thanksgiving early. They don't observe the holiday in China due to the lack of pilgrims, Native Americans, and Plymouth Rock. Shocker, I know." She shrugs nonchalantly.

"Right. Makes sense." The holiday info makes sense. Karie speaking flawless Chinese and having a foreign maiden name absolutely does not make sense.

She heaves another couple of bags in the back and I pass her a pillow. "The Chinese do, however, have a Mid-Autumn Festival. It's like Thanksgiving in that it celebrates a harvest and typically involves a family reunion. We dubbed it the 'Cho Family Mid-Autumn Festival of Thanksgiving' when Greg and I married." She smiles at the memory.

"So, you're adopted?" My words come out slowly as I piece some things together. "Oh! That picture of the happy Asian couple in your craft room. Those are your parents?" I wince, excited to solve the mystery but embarrassed to have ousted my ignorance. "They're such a cute couple. I thought you forgot to change the original picture. You know, the one that comes in the frame from the store?" Someone put a muzzle on me and save me from myself.

In her infinite kindness, she laughs a deep, giant belly laugh. "Oh my gosh, my parents are going to love you."

I let out a huge breath and grin.

Greg buckles Patrick into his car seat while the sleepy toddler spreads Pop-Tart crumbs all over the upholstery. Libby pulls out an iPad with a movie and a car game book and it looks like my plans to insert my EarPods, listen to Pie Takes the Cake, and doze off are officially canceled. I bet no one rests during a three-hour car ride with a wired eight-year-old and a lethargic toddler.

Mrs. Cho is my spirit animal. She's feisty, and I like it. And her fashion sense? She has a style all her own—a unique combination of vibrant prints and mismatched accessories that would make Taylor drool. If fashion is a form of self-expression, she definitely expresses herself with pride. Her loud pink sweater is adorable on her and she's wearing more bangles than I can count. I can't help but admire her confidence and individuality. I love her instantly and I want to be her when I grow up.

Dr. Cho? He has a way with words, but it doesn't seem like his hearing is quite up to par. When Greg or Karie tries to hold a conversation with him, he nods and smiles as if he understands every word, then responds with something completely unrelated. It's like watching a game of verbal charades. Libby tried to tell him about her cross-country season and ended up using hand gestures and exaggerated facial expressions to make sure he got the gist of what she was saying. Also, I have cousins–that's new! Karie has two siblings, also adopted, who have a few kids each, ranging in age from four to nineteen.

But the FOOD, oh my gosh, the food. I lost a few pounds over the past week, just not hungry when I think about losing Nonny, I guess. But huge platters of Kung Pao Chicken, Sweet and Sour Pork, and Cantonese Dim Sum are laid out on their massive dining room table, as well as a Lazy Susan rotating with generous serving spoons. I didn't realize I'd worried Karie so much, but when I put my fork down, I swear I see her breathe a sigh of relief.

When Mrs. Cho brings around the dessert–traditional Chinese mooncakes–I decide I'm not *that* full and thank her for not one, but two.

Stuffed, I lean back in my chair and rub my tummy. "You guys, I'm going to have a food baby."

Mrs. Cho chuckles, seemingly delighted that I'm so fond of her cooking. Greg, however, chokes on a potsticker and Karie gives him a swift, forceful pat on the back. Even Dr. Cho appreciates my statement and laughs at my funny. At least I think he appreciates it. It's hard to tell.

As we clean up after dinner, Mrs. Cho follows me into the kitchen with a huge stack of plates. I'm helping load the last of the glasses in the dishwasher when she leans in, cups my shoulder, and looks at me with soft features.

"Hadley, dear, I'm so sorry about the loss of your Nonny." Her kind smile is comforting, but I don't know when I'll stop feeling this tightness in my chest when someone mentions her.

"Thank you, Mrs. Cho."

"Please, call me NayNay."

I can't place the name to the emotion evoked by her request, but I can't manage to refer to Mrs. Cho as NayNay. Something about claiming a new grandparent makes me feel disloyal to Nonny. Even though I know Nonny would never be sad for me to welcome a loving person in my life. It's complicated.

When I hesitate to fulfill her request, she invites me to join her in the piano room. I learn all about the Chos. Dr. Cho is a retired radiologist; Mrs. Cho thinks he hears more than he lets on, but she plays along. Mrs. Cho is a biology teacher and when I tell her about my internship at Southern Salvage, she is impressed with their eco-friendly values and Christian principles.

"You know, Dr. Cho and I could never have biological children. Karie and her brothers, they have been such blessings. They made our family complete." I smile at her statement and, sensing she has more to add, nod so she'll continue.

"We're all adopted. My husband and I invited Karie into our family, God invites us all to his." Her expression and her soft tone give me the impression she doesn't say this to pressure me, but to make a simple statement.

"I'm a pretty big fan of Jesus, myself."

"But…" She says it more as a question.

This is hard to talk about, especially considering I've only known Mrs. Cho for a few hours. "But it's been a rough few months." I swallow the lump in my throat. "My Nonny reminded me constantly that God is good, no matter the circumstances. I always accepted that, it's just harder to live through difficult circumstances and still believe it." I bite my lip. "I feel terrible for saying that out loud." Please, tear ducts, please don't turn on now.

"Your Nonny was a wise woman." Mrs. Cho pats me on the knee. "And Hadley, God is big enough for your questions. Keep going to him. God works for the good of those who love him."

I take in a sharp breath, remembering my practice date with Colton just before Nonny passed away. "Romans 8:28. Colton said the same thing."

"Colton sounds wise too." She smiles.

Heat rises in my cheeks and travels all the way up to my ears, and Mrs. Cho doesn't fail to notice. "Hadley, dear, is there anything else you'd like to tell me about Colton?"

A giant grin splits my face. "Now, NayNay…"

And she cackles at my response.

Karie walks in as we rise, right in time to find me giving Mrs. Cho a side hug.

"Side-Hug-Hadley strikes again." I choke back a laugh and Karie shakes her head.

###

Later that evening, as the entire Kendall family settles into their makeshift beds and the pullout sofa in the family room, I take in the family pictures sitting on the mantle. Karie certainly has a beautiful, eclectic family. There are photographs of all three Cho children, not a single one resembling the other, but all with large, happy grins. Next to them stands a three-picture frame with each child on their "Gotcha" day and Ephesians 1:5 on the bottom of the frame. And then, mixed right in with the many photographs of the Cho grandchildren, is a four-by-six photo of me, Patrick, and Libby at Halloween. Warmth spreads through my chest.

With a full belly and a content heart, I sleep soundly for the first time in over a week.

CHAPTER 21

Simply A-Maize-Ing

》》 ———————————— 《《

...147, 148, 149.

Finally. All one hundred forty-nine lights are secured to the chandelier frame. I set my screwdriver and pliers down on the workbench, satisfied. Colton, who still manages to cause butterflies in my belly despite donning uber-dorky safety goggles, pulls his gloves off and throws them atop a pile of spare electrical wires and sockets.

"So, what are we naming this bad boy?" Colton moves his safety goggles to his forehead, the outline of the rims imprinted around his eyes. Still hot.

"Well, I was thinking *her* name could be Scintillant Soda." I peek at his face to gauge his reaction. He frowns, so I hurry to explain. "Raven suggested it in art class. It's a French word that means sparkle or shimmer. Or kind of like how a star might twinkle."

"I like it." He reassures me, the confused expression from moments before gone. Thank goodness. The alternative was "bottle beacon."

Mike saunters over in a hunter green Christmas shirt that says, "Dear Santa, I've been good(ish) this year." A truer shirt could never be found. He and Colton check the mounting bracket while Franny and I shuffle through drawers at the Waymaker station in search of wire nuts, connectors, and electrical tape. Franny turns the power off, then we secure the chandelier to its temporary home at Southern Salvage, where it'll stay until the Fall Festival this weekend. Franny turns the power back on and it takes my breath away. I can't speak for a moment, I'm so proud of my baby. A miniscule amount of moisture might be sneaking up under my eyelids.

"Stunning," I whisper, my voice full of reverence.

"Absolutely stunning," Colton says quietly, and it takes me a minute before I realize he isn't referring to the chandelier. Aware of his gaze fixed on me, I look away so he doesn't see me blush.

We've worked hard and the time has passed quickly. It's getting late. The glow of the moon shines in from the storefront windows.

"Walk you home?" Colton asks as he pulls the plug on the fixture. When I hesitate to leave, he chuckles. "She'll be fine, I promise."

"Sure, but shouldn't we take a few pictures for the Instagram account first?" There isn't enough room for the number of hashtags it would take me to adequately thank Bluegrass Bottlers, but that doesn't mean I can't try.

Franny, always one step ahead of us, is clicking and snapping photos from different angles and experimenting with various filters.

"She's got this taken care of." Colton opens the door for me, and we step out into the brisk November air. I zip my puffer jacket and decide I'm not quite bold enough to reach for his hand, so I shove mine in my pockets instead.

Colton walks me all the way to the front of the driveway and stops short of walking me to the door. It would be nice for the sidewalk to suddenly grow in length by a mile or ten. I do my best to hide my disappointment but smile when he waits until I'm safely inside and gives a wave when I open the door. Yep, I've got it bad.

###

Friday afternoon, we pull up to the barn at Broadwater Fairgrounds in the Southern Salvage van, the chandelier deconstructed in four large pieces. The building stands tall, with sturdy wooden planks and two heavy doors, reinforced with metal hinges and bolts. The inside is massive, the ceiling supported by heavy wooden beams–great for mounting a giant glass light fixture.

Like Southern Salvage, it's rustic but modern. The scent of hay and aged wood permeates the air. Colton, Mike, and I search the space to find Mr. Howardson. Standing near a stack of chairs, he seems out of place, clad

241

in a flannel shirt and overalls instead of his traditional khaki pants and button up shirt with sweater.

"My, my, Hadley, that may be the largest project BHS has ever had. Looked mighty fine on Instagram last night." I will not let it bother me that my elderly history teacher has social media and I don't. "Let me get the barn manager and you should be able to set up right in the center." He wanders off and we head back to the van to grab the project. We repeat the same process from before, and a sweaty hour later, "Scintillant Soda" is raised proudly at the center of the barn. Many of my classmates have started setting up their projects as well.

"Alright, students, please gather 'round and quiet down so we can discuss the process of the silent auction." Mr. Howardson dabs his forehead with a hanky. "I'm proud of all the hard work you and your mentors have put into this year's projects. If I were a betting man, I'd gather this might be a record-breaking year for the town trust. If you haven't already, please find your assigned table around the perimeter of the barn and display your work there. If your project is a service or event, you will need to display your required poster in lieu of the tangible item. All of you will need a clipboard with a bid sheet. Tomorrow, the auction will start at four p.m. and close at seven, right before the Native Husking Bee." Murmurs flow through the group. I've never heard of a Native Husking Bee, but it seems to be quite popular among my peers.

"Please wear your Sunday best and be at your table by three thirty p.m. tomorrow afternoon." With that, he wishes us good evening and we bustle off to continue readying our spaces.

The next afternoon, I can't bring myself to peek at anyone else's silent auction bid sheets.

There are so many amazing projects.

A girl who interned at the town bakery has made a three-layer cake with intricate designs in the icing. Peter interned with a photographer and has submitted framed black and white photographs of Broadwater landmarks. Another guy who interned at the hospital submitted a bid sheet for a free health screening event he organized with medical professionals. Raven, with her creative, artistic spirit, designed a fashionable dress using sustainable materials. She'll wear it for the auction tomorrow.

"You're thinking about the extra credit, aren't you?" Colton asks.

"Guilty," I fib. I doubt there are that many people interested in a giant light made of almost 150 glass bottles. Someone would have to own a massive house to even hang the thing. Actually, Kyra could probably fit it in her closet, but thou shalt not covet, so never mind.

I man my station and do my best to answer the festival goers' questions.

"Why, yes, I did score and cut all 149 bottles."

"I sure do have calluses after all that hard work."

"No, Mr. Sturgest isn't as scary as people make him out to be…"

Many people stop only to say hi to Colton. It seems he's a town celebrity.

Mayor Green steps to the podium on the makeshift stage at the front of the barn to make an announcement. "Ladies and gentlemen, thank you for attending this year's Broadwater Fall Festival. The silent auction is now closed. We will notify the winners of each item and announce the highest bid at the conclusion of the Husking Bee."

The barn buzzes with excitement as the mayor gestures for Mr. Howardson to take the microphone. He clears his throat and adjusts his glasses before he begins.

"Citizens of Broadwater, thank you again for coming out to this year's festival. It is now time for the Native Husking Bee." I'm not prepared for the thunderous applause that follows his announcement. "If you're new to our festival, this event is held in honor of our town founder, Jedediah Broadwater, and the agricultural community he and his family sustained early in our town's history. Known for his lighthearted personality, Jedediah appreciated a good harvest and a good time."

Someone in the audience wolf whistles and laughter erupts.

Mr. Howardson continues. "Originally from Nantucket, Jedediah brought the tradition of the native husking bee with him. We continue this meaningful event that combines both practicality and a celebration of community. We'd like to thank our local farmers for donating the corn this evening."

He pauses as town councilmen roll in four massive wheelbarrows full of corn, husks and all, to the front of the barn.

"Any single men in attendance are welcome to shuck the corn. Any gentleman who shucks a red ear of corn will receive a kiss from the lady of his choice—assuming she is a willing participant, of course." Mr. Howardson gives a stern look to the middle school boys lined up closest to the wheelbarrows. They bow their heads to conceal their snickering.

"Gentlemen, you may shuck to your heart's content." And then, it's organized mass chaos. Husks fly as men and boys tear into the piles of corn. My jaw nearly hits the floor when I watch Colton roll up his sleeves, lock eyes with mine, and raise a brow in friendly challenge. Just as he elbows his way into the masses, Peter Staton holds up an ear of red corn. Peter scans the crowd until his eyes land on... Kyra.

Huh. I did *not* see that coming.

When Kyra sees Peter start to make his way over, she shakes her head no, but she's smiling. She turns to run, but, as everyone can clearly tell, just slow enough to allow him to catch up with her. They lock lips and the crowd devolves into hoots and hollers, especially when Peter pumps his corn filled fist in victory, mid-smooch.

As quickly as the event began, it concludes. The councilmen return with brooms and start to sweep up the husks as Mr. Howardson returns to the microphone.

"Well done, Mr. Staton. Students, congratulations on the successful sale of your auction items. Together, you raised over $50,000 for the Broadwater Community Trust, a record! We'd also like to thank our community business partners for sponsoring and mentoring our students. We couldn't do this without you." Polite applause fills the barn.

"Tonight's highest bid was made by an anonymous buyer. Totaling $6,501, Scintillant Soda by Hadley Edwards, sponsored by Southern Salvage and under the guidance of her mentor Colton Sturgest, has won best project."

Stunned, I freeze. Mike shakes my shoulders as others around me applaud, and Colton has a grin so wide I wonder if it might actually split his face.

###

The night winds down and the crowd dwindles. Many of the other projects have gone home with their buyers. Mr. Howardson instructed me and Colton to leave the chandelier hanging in the barn–buyer request–and said he'd give me the information about the *Broadwater Beacon Magazine* interview next week at school.

Mike walks up to us and gives Colton a brown paper bag.

"Always clutch, Uncle Mike. Thank you." Colton crinkles the top of the bag shut and gives me a grin.

"What's in the bag?" I ask, curious.

"So nosy." He tsks. "You'll have to wait and see. It's something special for later."

"Later, huh?" This kind of feels a bit like flirting.

"Yeah, later." That smile is definitely flirtatious. "Right after we return the van to the store."

Right.

I stifle a yawn as Colton pulls the van into the parking lot at Southern Salvage. "Hadley, can I walk you home?" His tone is more serious than before.

"Yeah, I'd like that." Who wouldn't?

The van beeps as Colton locks it with the key fob, then his hand is at the small of my back, where it remains as we walk in companionable silence. This time Colton doesn't stop at the fence, he walks all the way to the door, then reaches for my hand and gives a gentle squeeze. He doesn't let go but looks me straight in the eye. I glance at the bag quizzically, then back to him. He returns my gaze with a hint of mischief in his eyes. And a touch of something else?

"Hadley, this is for you."

I eye the bag again and his hand goes behind his neck. He looks so vulnerable.

"But… but I don't have anything for you." My stomach drops. Is gift giving between a mentor and mentee a custom someone forgot to tell me about?

"I don't need anything. I just want to give you this."

My heart races in my chest as I pull the edges of the bag back. Inside is a single ear of red corn. I bite my bottom lip to hide my grin. I'm sure I'm blushing but I don't care.

Colton's eyes–darker blue in the dim glow of the porch light–search mine. "Is this okay with you, Hadley?" he asks, his voice low as he steps a fraction of an inch closer. He really is a beautiful person.

"Mm-hmm." I give a subtle nod and he leans in, his head tilting slightly to the side. His fingers caress my jawline, and his soft lips touch mine. He kisses me gently at first, then increases the pressure. It feels like time passes blissfully slow, but the kiss ends and I want to rewind, feeling as though the moment passed too quickly.

"So much better than a Hershey's," I joke. "Is it one kiss for every ear of corn or for each kernel?"

He laughs, a wonderful sound, then we kiss again.

And again.

"Thank you for helping me, Hadley."

"Hmm?" I gaze up at him, not sure what he means.

"For helping me open up. You made me smile again. You make me smile all the time."

Hearing that makes *me* smile and I reach up on my toes to kiss him one last time before he has to leave.

"Goodnight Hadley," Colton whispers, and places another small kiss on my forehead.

"Goodnight Colton."

A swoon worthy dimple marks his cheek as he backs toward the street. When I slip inside, the second I close the door behind me, Libby starts singing, "Colton and Hadley, sitting in a tree, K-I-S-S-I-N-G…" My cheeks burn. I turn and find even Karie is wearing a knowing grin on her face.

I don't try to hide my smile as I walk on air all the way up the stairs, poke my head in Patrick's room to say goodnight, and head to the shower. When I've dried off and dressed in my jammies, I'm surprised to find Greg sitting stiffly on the edge of my bed.

"Have a seat, Hadley." He motions to the chair at my desk and I think we're about to have a little moment. He clears his throat. Twice. "Uh, Hadley…" He shifts in his seat, then crosses and uncrosses his arm. This is so awkward for him, for both of us. It's worse than the time he had to ask my birth date in the emergency room lobby. I wait. "Karie told me about Colton walking you home, and I can only guess by Libby's four encore performances of the K-I-S-S-I-N-G song that you two are more than just friends."

A flush creeps across my face and I bite the inside of my cheek to keep from smiling.

"Right. Well, Colton's a good kid, a great kid." He clears his throat again. "You know, I don't mean to sound hypocritical to the daughter I made at seventeen…" As he tapers off in search of the right words, I discover where my propensity for blushing comes from. I'm sure we're both the same deep shade of red.

"I make good choices, Dad."

His head snaps up at this term of endearment, a smile growing on his face.

"Yeah, I've picked up on that," he acknowledges. "One of my favorite books is Rick Warren's *The Purpose of Christmas*, I read it every December—you can borrow it, if you want. I started reading it again last night and a line I never paid much attention to stuck out to me. 'There are accidental parents, but no accidental babies.'" He gets choked up and I'm not sure what to say, so I remain quiet, and he continues.

"When your grandmother called me in August, I had no idea she was going to tell me I had a daughter. I was scared, Hadley. Terrified. I didn't know what to expect, but you've been such a blessing. I'm glad you're here, and it's no mistake you are."

My eyes prickle and I give him an infamous side hug.

"You have to keep your door open any time Colton comes over, you know that right?"

Of course he says that. It takes sheer willpower not to roll my eyes when I respond, "Yes sir," but I appreciate his dad-ness, no matter how awkward it might feel. Before he leaves, he turns and says, "Your grandmother would have been very proud of you tonight. And every night."

Of course I have to Facetime Taylor. I give her the full report, and we squeal like little girls when I recall Colton's kisses.

CHAPTER 22

God is Still Good

》》 ———————————— 《《

I like to joke that food is my love language, but it's really gift-giving. But bonus points if the gift is food. I made a digital copy of Mr. Strugests' Veteran's Day photo and had it enlarged on canvas as a thank you for taking me on as an intern. On Friday evening I approach the front door only to see a sign that says, "*Closed Early Today.*" Confused, I reach for my phone to text Colton but see Mike making goofy faces in the window. He unlocks the door and shows me in, Vannah White style. I follow Mike to the back of the dark store, past several dimly lit Christmas trees, when suddenly, the lights flick on and everyone yells, "Surprise!"

I gape at the Southern Salvage staff. They're standing around a long table made from reclaimed wooden bowling lanes with the polished "Broadwater Bowling" logo buffed to a shine right in the middle. A "Congratulations" banner is hung in the background.

"This shindig is all in your honor," Mike informs me, proud as a peacock. "We're celebrating your successful internship." He pats me on the back. "And Colton," he says, as his nephew walks over and stands beside me. "Boy, you must have been real good this year for Santa to bring you a girlfriend."

"I'm at the top of the nice list, like always." He weaves his fingers through mine and gives a little squeeze. Does he feel the same electric jolt I do when we touch? Neither one of us bothers to correct Mike after he refers to me as Colton's girlfriend, and I grow lightheaded with the potential relationship upgrade. "Come on, girlfriend." Swoon.

Oh! There's a sweet tea fountain. And pizza. And brownies.

Drool.

I hand Mr. Sturgest his gift and card after he pulls out a chair for me at the table, next to Colton, of course.

"Oh, my goodness, you guys, you didn't have to do all this." I press my fingers to my smiling lips. "Thank you." My heart is so full it may burst.

There are even a few gifts. Mike presents me with a shirt that says "Not a Hugger" with a screen-printed cactus. "It fits, and *it fits*!" he says, obviously proud of himself.

Franny hands me a gift certificate to El Restaurante Increíble and assures me that the fish tacos really are worth a try. Hard pass, but I don't tell her that. When I unwrap the gift from Colton, I'm touched to find a double frame featuring a printed photograph of our first Instagram picture together and what appears to be a... no, it couldn't be... could it?

"I used the printing press to make that poster you wanted to make the first time we met. Proverbs 3:5-6, right?" He toys with his watch and offers a nervous smile.

"Right." I smile, touched. "I already know where I'm going to put this on my desk." He kisses my forehead, and we turn our attention to the food.

We eat and we celebrate, and then we eat some more. But as all great things must come to an end, I thank everyone and excuse myself. I have a huge presentation tomorrow and I want to be ready.

Colton walks me home and I kiss my boyfriend goodnight.

Sigh.

I don't think this will ever get old.

###

I'm nervous, but not anxious—and let me tell you, there is a difference. My big Presentation of Learning is scheduled for Friday in the BHS Library Media Center. Colton and Franny have been helping me choose pictures to include in the slideshow while Taylor and Libby are helping me select my outfit. By "select my outfit," I mean I had to try on FIVE ensembles and model them with different shoes while they offered commentary like some panel of self-important judges on a Netflix reality fashion show. That said, insta-sis is being extra-adorable, trying on my clothes and lip-gloss as we Facetime my Annapolis BFF. We settle on simple black dress pants, a fuchsia sweater because "blondes should always wear pink" according to my eight-year-old sister, and flats. My jewelry loving bestie suggested keeping the accessories simple, which shocked me.

I don't sleep a wink.

The next morning, I gather my notes in the BHS library. My insta-family, all of them, attend the Presentation of Learning–even Libby is checked out of school–as does Colton and most of the Southern Salvage staff, all except for Mike. They really left the goofiest one of the bunch, the fun-loving, absent-minded uncle, in charge at the store. No one but me seems the least bit nervous about this. Even Dr. and Mrs. Cho make it.

I sit politely through my classmates' presentations, but it's hard to focus with my nerves, except when the bakery intern passes out cannolis. I have zero trouble focusing on that portion of the presentation.

And then, I'm up. I stand at the front and clear my throat, which is exactly what Mr. Howardson recommended we not do. Oops.

"Peers, Community Members, BHS Staff,

It has been an honor to serve as a mentee with Southern Salvage, and I'm so grateful to the Sturgest family for allowing me to intern. Thank you for your guidance and support. Each of you, especially Colton," cue the blush, "have selflessly shared your wealth of knowledge and experience, patiently guiding me through the highs and lows of creating a giant chandelier out of soda bottles, and you've shown me what it means to be resilient, to persevere in the face of challenges, and to embrace failure as a steppingstone to success.

"Mr. Sturgest and Mr. Howardson, I'm indebted to both of you for the countless hours you've invested in me, the invaluable advice you've provided, and for pushing me to surpass my own limitations. You've believed in me even when I doubted my ability to work in the field of antiques—you encouraged me to step outside my comfort zone and embrace new opportunities for growth. You both seemed to see something in me I couldn't see in myself, and I will be forever grateful for that.

"When I started at BHS in the fall, I was unaware of the internship requirement. I was in the process of applying for another internship program to honor my grandfather's career with the U.S. Navy—it was supposed to be an effort to honor him and his hopes and dreams for me. But he would have preferred me to honor him by pursuing something I'm passionate about to the best of my ability. I'm pleased to report that this upcoming summer I've accepted an internship position with the Kentucky Historical Society in Frankfort. I'll be working in their children's department, and I'd be lying if I said I wasn't excited about it."

The weight that lifts off my shoulders when I announce this is incredible. I glance at Colton and he's grinning from ear to ear and can't help but show his excitement about this revelation. Mr. Howardson looks pretty pumped too, the program relating to history and all. He helped keep my secret, after all. He even wrote my recommendation letter.

"I also want to thank the Kendalls, my family, for welcoming me so wholeheartedly and encouraging me during my internship. You guys, Mr. Howardson, the Sturgests, Colton, you've all helped me find acceptance and belonging. I thought a lot about what I wanted to say today…ugh, I really didn't want to tear up." I stop for a second to fish a tissue from my pocket and blot my eyes.

"I know this isn't a customary part of the presentation, but I want to explain that I didn't come to Broadwater under ideal circumstances. I came because my Nonny was sick and she wanted me to stay with my father and his family, whom I'd never met. I miss her. I will always miss my Nonny. But God works in some crazy ways." I have to pause again. I'm a blubbering, snotty mess.

Get it together, Hadley. Deep breath.

"God has been moving in my life through this project. Through my internship with the Sturgests and my relationship with my family—the Kendalls and the Chos— I've learned that we're all 'salvaged' treasures. I didn't know who I was if I wasn't trying to honor my grandfather's legacy, or Nonny's granddaughter, Taylor's best friend, many things. But family and friends I've come to care for shared scripture with me, verses like Romans 8:28, 2 Corinthians 5:17, and Ephesians 1:5. I'm confident in my identity as a child of God. You and I don't have to earn love or fit a mold. We're all adopted children in the kingdom of God, and we've been *salvaged* by a Savior, Jesus. Like the light that is given off by Scintillant Soda, I want my light to shine for him."

My audience, the ones that paid attention, are either cheesing big time or leaking from their eyeballs like me. But I'm done. I did it.

"Thank you everyone."

Behind me, on the giant smart screen television, images of the giant coke-bottle chandelier fade to other pictures, one of me biting my lip but gritting out a smile as I pose for the Instagram photo displaying the gnarly cut on my hand, an image of me and Colton on the cover of the Broadwater Beacon magazine in front of Scintillant Soda, even one of my reluctantly soft-hearted boss smiling at me. The slideshow concludes with me beaming at the camera while Colton gazes at me during the Fall Festival.

How is it possible to feel the high of relief from a tough job well done, and exhausted all at the same time?

During the refreshments afterward, Patrick spills juice all over my sweater and I'm forced to change into my cactus shirt. I get a few funny looks, but…

God is still good.

Always.

Thank you so much for reading *Salvaged*. Please take a moment to leave a quick review. Reviews help others find this story. I appreciate you!

If you'd like more contemporary young adult Christian fiction, please visit www.shannamheath.com

Acknowledgements

Dear Reader,

I am so grateful to all those who have journeyed with me through the creation of this novel. Writing *Salvaged* was a labor of love, and I extend my deepest appreciation to the One who inspires all creativity – the Author of Life.

There are SO many people to thank. My husband, Jeff, my children, Abigail, Miriam, and Owen, and my parents. Your encouragement, patience, and understanding have been a Godsend, and I am blessed to have you in my life.

Sincere thanks to my Bible study buddy/accountability partner/prayer warrior/designer of the beautiful cover of this book, Ashley Feather. Your friendship is a blessing!

To my critique group at the American Christian Fiction Writers, I thank you for your unwavering support and for being the pillars that kept me grounded. Your belief in this project has meant more to me than words can express. To Angela D. Shelton, Lauren Thell, Lisa Phillips, and Michelle Sanchez—Thank you for your thoughtful, insightful comments (and for not being afraid to hurt my feelings!).

Thank you to my Sisters-in-Christ through the Refresh Group at Calvary Baptist Church for your prayers and encouragement. You are all a constant source of inspiration and strength. I love you, ladies!

To my editor, Leilani, whose keen insight and guidance helped shape this story into what it is today— please know that your expertise was invaluable and much appreciated.

To my readers, young and young-at-heart, thank you for giving this story a place in your hearts. It is my sincere hope that amidst the twists and turns, you found moments of inspiration, reflection, and, above all, a deeper connection to the divine. I pray *Salvaged* has been a source of joy, faith, and growth for each of you.

Above all, I give thanks to God, from whom all blessings flow.

Blessings,

Shanna M. Heath

Made in the USA
Columbia, SC
22 February 2024

31902210R00162